C0-APO-710

"HOW COULD YOU LIE TO ME, BRIT?" HARRISON DEMANDED.

"How could you make love to me and all the while be spying on me? Is learning the secret to my robot that important to you?"

Tears flooded Brit's eyes. "I didn't lie—not exactly. But as long as we're accusing each other, how could you make love to me, share what we shared, and call it *infatuation?* You're just like one of your machines, Harrison. You're the Tin Man in *The Wizard of Oz*—no heart."

"That's ridiculous!"

"Is it? You've turned yourself into a machine, and you expect me to be one, too. Handy to have around but no feelings. Not that it matters anymore," she choked out. "Now that you've got your precious Wonder Woman robot, let her warm your bed!"

CANDLELIGHT ECSTASY CLASSIC ROMANCES

CANDLELIGHT ECSTASY ROMANCES®

QUANTITY SALES

Most Dell Books are available at special quantity discounts when purchased in bulk by corporations, organizations, and special-interest groups. Custom imprinting or excerpting can also be done to fit special needs. For details write: Dell Publishing Co., Inc., 1 Dag Hammarskjold Plaza, New York, NY 10017, Attn.: Special Sales Dept., or phone: (212) 605-3319.

INDIVIDUAL SALES

Are there any Dell Books you want but cannot find in your local stores? If so, you can order them directly from us. You can get any Dell book in print. Simply include the book's title, author, and ISBN number, if you have it, along with a check or money order (no cash can be accepted) for the full retail price plus 75¢ per copy to cover shipping and handling. Mail to: Dell Readers Service, Dept. FM, P.O. Box 1000, Pine Brook, NJ 07058.

THE QUINTESSENTIAL WOMAN

Cory Kenyon

A CANDLELIGHT ECSTASY ROMANCE®

Published by
Dell Publishing Co., Inc.
1 Dag Hammarskjold Plaza
New York, New York 10017

Copyright © 1987 by Mary Tate Engels and Vicki Lewis
Thompson

All rights reserved. No part of this book may be reproduced or
transmitted in any form or by any means, electronic or
mechanical, including photocopying, recording, or by any
information storage and retrieval system, without the written
permission of the Publisher, except where permitted by law.

Dell ® TM 681510, Dell Publishing Co., Inc.

Candlelight Ecstasy Romance®, 1,203,540, is a registered
trademark of Dell Publishing Co., Inc., New York, New York.

ISBN: 0-440-17218-7

Printed in the United States of America

March 1987

10 9 8 7 6 5 4 3 2 1

WFH

To Audrey, Brent, Nathan, Noel, and Shane,
whose whirlwind presence and frenzied activity
inspired The Quintessential Woman

To Our Readers:

We have been delighted with your enthusiastic response to Candlelight Ecstasy Romances®, and we thank you for the interest you have shown in this exciting series.

In the upcoming months we will continue to present the distinctive sensuous love stories you have come to expect only from Ecstasy. We look forward to bringing you many more books from your favorite authors and also the very finest work from new authors of contemporary romantic fiction.

As always, we are striving to present the unique, absorbing love stories that you enjoy most—books that are more than ordinary romance. Your suggestions and comments are always welcome. Please write to us at the address below.

Sincerely,

The Editors
Candlelight Romances
1 Dag Hammarskjold Plaza
New York, New York 10017

THE
QUINTESSENTIAL
WOMAN

CHAPTER ONE

Brit McIver stood poised for battle.

Her enemy, Harrison Kent, held the power to destroy her business. As far as Brit was concerned, the battle lines had been drawn the moment he opened his mouth during that TV interview. She had to fight back to save her livelihood. It was a matter of survival.

Her first line of defense had been to infiltrate the enemy camp and set up a spy network. Now—search and destroy! Casually dressed for the fight, she wore a buff wool sweater over a black cotton turtleneck with a brown leather belt. Her khaki slacks were stuffed into chestnut suede pant-boots, and her swinging blond hair was drawn back from her heart-shaped face by a paisley scarf.

Brit paused for a moment outside his door and caught the animated sounds of Saturday morning cartoons coming from inside the house. *"What's up, doc?"* She smiled to herself. Okay, Mr. Hotsie-Totsie Inventor, I'm about to see what's up.

She should have suspected that this was not a normal household when she heard the doorbell play the first four bars of "Rocky." But she was so intent on her mission that when the door swung open, she launched into her best sales pitch.

"Congratulations. The Quintessential Woman wants you! She wants to give you a special gift—a free housecleaning. The Quintessential Woman is unique and complete. She cleans, caters, even baby-sits, and she can organize your home into a smooth, well-oiled machine."

"There aren't any babies around here, and we have enough machines. Does she do windows? How about floors? Can she cook?"

Brit McIver stared dumbly at the lanky, sandy-haired kid opposite her. He looked to be about eleven or twelve. His brown eyes gazed steadily back at her, making an assessment. Drat! She'd given her spiel to the wrong person. "Of course we do windows," she replied. "We do anything that needs doing around a house."

"We won a free house?" a pipsqueak voice chimed.

Brit's gaze fell upon a little girl who was peeping beneath the lanky kid's arm. The child was beautiful, with golden curls entangled around her shoulders and innocent blue eyes. A large circle of red lipstick outlined her mouth, and yards of purple chiffon draped her small body. She tottered in a pair of black high heels.

"Not a free house," Brit explained patiently. "A free house cleaning. Look, is your mother home?"

"No, but my dad is," the boy answered. "And he might be interested in getting this place cleaned. It's a wreck."

"Mommy's gone to heaven," the little girl piped up again.

The boy groaned. "Avery, you don't have to tell every stranger. Dad said that's a private matter."

"Well, I miss her," the child pouted.

"How could you miss her? You were only two when it happened. You don't even remember her."

"Do too! You don't know everything, Shane." The child swooped away, dragging her purple chiffon tail.

A pang of sympathy for the motherless children shot through Brit. She quickly appealed to the young boy. "If your father's home, could I please see him?"

"Sure. Come on. He's up here." The kid did exactly as she requested. He took her to see his father.

Brit followed the boy called Shane into the attractive but rather messy home and was immediately startled by a strange yelping sound at her heels. "Aag!"

"Don't worry, she won't bite. She just barks." Avery's pixie face reappeared around the corner. "This is Cuddles, my guard dog."

"Poodles can't be guard dogs. They're too curly and little. A guard dog has to be big." Shane scoffed at his small sister.

"Can too!" Avery drew herself up to rebuff her tall brother. "Cuddles can be a guard dog if I want her to be. All I have to do is program her to the Bark Mode."

"Wait a minute!" Brit interrupted. "I don't know what you two are arguing about. That's not even a real dog!" She studied the blustering metal creature that had curly tufts glued to what resembled a head and a waggly wire tail. "But what is it?"

"Oh, Avery wanted a puppy," Shane explained. "But Dad says he has enough mouths to feed with all of us. So he made her one that doesn't have to eat."

"There are more kids?" Brit was beginning to get the picture. And a strange picture it was.

"Just a brother. Avery, would you please put that thing in the Go-Sleep Mode so it'll stop barking?"

"I don't want to. Today she's my guard dog."

They left the furry creature yelping in the foyer and mounted the stairs. Brit noticed toys left dangerously on the steps, three broken banister rails, and stains spotting the carpet. So this was the home of Harrison Kent. Her enemy. Somehow, she hadn't pictured him living in suburban Virginia with kids running rampant through an average split-level house. She'd imagined him tucked away in an elite walk-up in Alexandria.

Ah, but this was much better for her plan. From all appearances, the Kent household desperately needed her services.

Earlier, as Brit was driving over the Potomac searching out the man's hostile encampment, she appreciated why so many people chose to live in Vienna, a lovely wooded suburb near the nation's capital. When the trees bloomed in the springtime, the place must be gorgeous, she thought. One definitely had a feeling of being in a country setting, nowhere near the headquarters of an electronic wizard.

The sandy-haired youth led her into a room at the

14

end of the hall. Brit followed briskly, and Avery trailed along behind, her purple chiffon gown dragging on the steps. Fleetingly, Brit thought they might be going to a bedroom; then she decided it would be the father's office. Surely the kids wouldn't lead her into his bedroom. . . .

Brit stopped short as she entered the room. *These* kids had done just that. She faced a darkly handsome man wrapped only in a burgundy towel. Her enemy in the raw.

Harrison Kent looked up when his eleven-year-old son, Shane, entered the room. He immediately decided that another family council was in order to remind the kids once again about privacy in the bedroom, especially in his bedroom.

In this uninhibited family, it wasn't unusual for him to pull back the shower curtain and discover Avery and two of her little girl friends playing behind it. Or to awaken from a dead sleep to face a troop of neighborhood kids and one of the boys asking, "Dad, can I show them how Squeegee cleans the windows?" or "Can the kids see how Felix picks up clothes and sorts them for the laundry?"

Now Harrison noticed that Shane was being followed by a fuzzy entourage. *Fuzzy* because without his glasses, Harrison couldn't distinguish faces from a distance. He did, however, recognize his small daughter. She was shorter than anyone else and usually wore some strange outfit that dragged along the floor or balanced on her head. The other figure was several inches taller than Shane—probably one of Shane's buddies who was experiencing a sudden surge of hormones that had shot his young body

15

from four feet one to five feet six inches in height overnight.

"Shane, please, son. Tell your friend no robot demonstrations now. I don't have time. I have a million things to do before tonight."

"But Dad, this is—"

Harrison waved his hand to stop Shane's protest. "Not today, Shane." He turned away and reached into the closet.

Brit gulped at the sight of the extremely masculine body exhibited so gloriously before her. His bare flesh still glistened with moisture from a shower, and tiny droplets clung to the curly smattering of dark hair across the muscular chest. She found herself admiring this man who was her enemy.

As Brit was working to maintain her composure, Harrison Kent started pulling clothes out of the closet and spreading them on the bed. "Shane, would you do me a big favor? Shine my black shoes. Or should I wear brown tonight? What do you think? Maybe the brown ones?"

"Black is more powerful." The words spilled out before Brit could stop them, then she quickly pressed the tips of her fingers to her lips. The man whose crazy inventions might well ruin her business looked up and squinted beautiful ebony eyes at her.

Harrison Kent blinked at the stranger. Closer inspection revealed an attractive young woman standing in his bedroom, and he had absolutely no idea who she was! She definitely was not one of Shane's buddies. Swiftly, he grabbed a royal blue velvet robe and wrapped it around his gorgeous half-naked body. "Who are you? And what are you doing in here?"

"I—" Brit gestured helplessly at Shane. "I asked to see their father. I had no idea they were bringing me here."

Her attempt at an apology made the man laugh. "Sometimes my kids just don't think a situation through and consider whether I'm dressed for company. Anyway, thanks for the advice. You're right about the shoes. Black would be better. Uh, what kind of tie?"

"I like this one, Daddy." Avery whipped a red tie from the closet floor and draped it around her own neck. "See? Aren't I pretty?"

"You're beautiful, pepper. What color is it?" He leaned closer to scrutinize the item, and his blue robe parted to reveal a strong brown chest.

Brit's eyes admired—then darted away from—that stretch of masculine flesh.

"It's red, my favorite color." The child kicked off her high heels and danced around the room.

Shane picked up a pair of shoes. "The black ones, Dad?"

Harrison nodded. "If she says so. She seems to have good taste. Now, what are you selling, young lady?"

Shane walked past his father with a nod in Brit's direction. "She wants you, Dad. She knows a woman with a funny-sounding name who wants to clean the house." He took the shoes into an adjoining room, presumably the bathroom. "She does windows and floors. Says she can cook, too."

Brit realized that if she didn't gather her wits and

make her own statement, these precocious kids would do it for her. The only thing she could think to say to this man as he stood before her practically nude was her memorized speech.

"Congratulations, sir. The Quintessential Woman wants you. She wants to give you a special gift—a free house cleaning. The Quintessential Woman does everything from cleaning to catering to baby— er, child-sitting. In no time, she can have your household humming like a well-oiled . . . uh, machine." Her traitorous eyes dropped as she thought of his glistening chest.

"A well-oiled machine, huh?" He nodded briskly. "I like that."

Brit gulped and tried to pretend she wasn't staring at the handsome man. Actually, he himself had looked like a well-oiled machine wrapped in that towel. Fumbling in her purse, she handed him a brochure.

But he refused it. "I don't have time to read it. Just tell me what you want."

"Free house, tree house," Avery sang as she danced around her father, trailing her small hands around his bare legs. "Daddy! You're still wet!"

"Avery, darling, please let me talk to this lady." He squinted at Brit. "You clean houses?"

"The Quintessential Woman does more than clean houses, sir. She is a unique and complete home management service, offering to fill whatever needs your family has." Brit laid the brochure on the dresser. "Actually, I can come back some other time when it's more convenient."

18

"I could use someone to clean the house," he said. "Can you do it now?"

"Now?" She gasped. "It's a little late to get someone to come in today, but I could arrange it first thing Monday."

"I thought you said you did it."

"Well, I organize it. I have a full staff who can do anything you need."

"She can cook, Dad." Shane called.

"You can?" Harrison gave her another squinty-eyed look.

"Certainly, sir. The Quintessential Woman has a fine French chef."

Avery stopped dancing. "Can he make pancakes?"

"French chefs don't make pancakes, stupid!" Shane called loudly. "They make crêpes."

"Daddy, he called me stupid!"

Harrison Kent placed a large hand on his daughter's head. "But we all know you aren't stupid. Don't pay any attention to him, Avery." He addressed Brit. "You sure you can't stay now and clean the house?"

"Well, I don't usually—"

The phone rang, and little Avery dashed to the bedside table, lifted the receiver, and began to chatter. Harrison ignored her conversation and turned back to Brit. "I need someone now. I'm having important guests tonight, and my current housekeeper quit yesterday."

"She only lasted two weeks," Shane called from out of sight. "But that's more than most."

"Shane!" Harrison's voice was sharp.

19

"It's the truth," Shane mumbled.

"Enough!" Harrison snapped, then softened his voice for Brit. "Wouldn't you consider just staying on for a few hours? I really need someone—"

"Daddy! It's for you." Avery brought the cordless phone to him. "This lady says everybody's sick and she can't cater tonight."

"What?" He grabbed the phone from his daughter, panic already lighting his dark eyes. "Yes, this is Harrison Kent. What do you mean you can't come tonight? Yes, yes, I know what hepatitis is. . . . No, I certainly do not want any of your staff handling food around here. Well, can you send someone else? You have an obligation to me, you know!" Finally, he gave up and handed the phone back to Avery. "Well, there goes dinner tonight. If I can't find a caterer quick, I'll be serving pizza on bone china."

Shane appeared in the far doorway. "Dad, you can't serve pizza to the investors. They're too important."

Harrison braced his fists on his slim hips. "Do you have any bright ideas?"

"What about her?" Shane gestured toward Brit.

"I can make my favorite Marshmallow Surprise for your party tonight, Daddy," Avery offered.

"No, thanks, pepper. Daddy needs—"

A loud explosion from outside rattled the windows.

"What the hell was that?" Harrison started across the room. "Where's Murphy? Where are my glasses?"

"It's probably Murph the Smurf with another one

20

of his crazy experiments," Shane said, rushing from the room.

Avery followed, chanting, "Murph the Smurf. Murph the Smurf."

A pair of glasses lay on the dresser beside Brit's brochure, and she quickly handed them to Harrison. "These yours?"

"Yes, thanks." He grabbed the glasses and stuck them on while he dashed downstairs, still wearing his robe.

Brit saw no other recourse than to troop after them, avoiding the dangerously abandoned toys on the stairs, past the still-yelping robot dog in the foyer. In the backyard another boy, much shorter than Shane, stood before a smoking bottle. His dark mahogany hair was singed in the front and his eyebrows and eyelashes were short stubbles. By some miracle, the boy hadn't been seriously hurt by the accident.

He looked up guiltily at his father. "It backfired," he said weakly.

But Harrison Kent had a good deal to say. After he had finished a tirade on safety and experiments with matches and playing with dangerous toys, he sent poor Murphy to his room, Avery to watch TV, and Shane to finish shining the shoes. Then he wheeled around and faced Brit, seeing her clearly with his glasses for the first time. "You still here?"

"I'm glad he wasn't hurt in that explosion, Mr. Kent," Brit replied evenly. "Children can get themselves into serious trouble sometimes. And you really should keep the clutter off those stairs, too. That's an accident just waiting to happen."

"Now look," he grated. "So far, this hasn't been a terrific morning. My kid nearly blew his head off with some damned experiment; my maid quit and the house looks like a tornado whipped through it; my caterer's cook has hepatitis; and I have six guests coming to dinner who could make or break my entire future. I don't need you to tell me how to take care of my family."

At that instant, Brit made her decision. In her opinion he did need her, and she would be a fool not to seize the opportunity. She smiled serenely and cooed, "What you need, Mr. Kent, is the Quintessential Woman."

Her fresh-scrubbed beauty struck Harrison Kent, and for a moment he gaped at her. The March wind rustled through bare branches, and he shivered involuntarily. "Before we catch pneumonia, why don't we go inside and talk about this?"

Brit's blue-green eyes flickered with triumph as they walked back into the house.

Harrison Kent followed the attractive young woman into his own house. She was the most poised, unflappable person he'd met in a long time. It was definitely an admirable trait to have around. Actually, it was great.

"The Quintessential Woman will soon have your household humming like a well-oiled machine, Mr. Kent."

He looked at her with frank admiration. "You mean, you'll do it? You'll clean it today?"

"We'll do everything. Clean. Cook. Serve your guests. Clean up afterward. And watch your children."

22

"All that? A few minutes ago, you said you couldn't get anyone to work on such short notice."

Brit smiled indulgently. "I'll take this project myself. And I do have an emergency crew for dire circumstances. In the light of everything that's happened—er, is happening—I think you qualify. Now, you just show me where everything is, and I'll take care of the rest." She smiled to herself. This was going to be easier than she had originally thought. Now all she had to do was pull it off tonight, make him eternally grateful to the Quintessential Woman, and get his signature for a long-term commitment.

Mission complete. Infiltration accomplished. She would have frequent access to her enemy's quarters. The initial feat, of course, was to organize this chaos and make the evening a success. Quite a challenge. But the Quintessential Woman could do anything.

"First," she instructed, "show me only the rooms that will be used for entertaining your guests tonight. We'll concentrate on them. Then the kitchen. And may I use the phone? I need to call in my resources."

He did as she requested—still clad only in that beautiful blue robe. Opening the hall closet, he said, "Cleaning equipment is in here. We have a few mechanical resources of our own. Here's the vacuum cleaner. The kids call it Bumpy."

Brit gaped at the funny-looking tub-shaped machine. "Where's the handle?"

"You don't need one. Bumpy steers himself." He pushed a button, and the weird vacuum cleaner started off down the hall.

"I can see why the kids call it Bumpy. It bumps into everything," she observed wryly.

"He's sensory oriented," Harrison explained simply, as if anyone would understand that logic.

"It is kind of amazing," Brit muttered as she watched the thing bump its way along and disappear into the living room. "No wonder the furniture looks like—well, never mind. I can manage."

"If you need help, just ask one of the kids. They know how to work all the robotics around here. I have plenty to do before tonight. And thanks so much, Ms. uh—"

Brit gripped his warm extended hand and for the moment completely forgot he was the enemy. But she quickly recovered. "I'm Brit McIver. Brit," she added with a self-assured smile.

"The Quintessential Woman," he murmured in admiration, his ebony eyes meeting hers steadily. "I'm Harrison Kent. Harrison." He returned the smile and clung to her hand for a moment longer.

"I know. I mean, I saw you on TV last week talking about your newest invention. The multieverything robot."

"Ah." He nodded and immediately lapsed into another language. "The multidigital latitudinarian scope robot. Actually it isn't built yet. Still in the schematic stage. In fact, that's why I've invited these people here tonight. They're potential investors who are coming to see an exhibit of the small prototype. Based on its performance and the prospectus data, they could make the robot a reality by providing the capital for its full creation and production."

24

"I can see how important this evening is to you," Brit said. "Don't worry about a thing, Harrison. The Quintessential Woman can handle everything."

"I'm sure you can, Brit." His dark eyes lingered a moment longer. "And thanks again."

Brit watched as the robot wizard darted back upstairs, pausing to grab a few of the abandoned toys along the way.

She smiled involuntarily. Harrison Kent wasn't so bad, as enemies go. Dark and handsome. Black mysterious eyes that revealed a touch of warmth— just a touch. An angular face with nice lines and a shadow of a beard. He also had a very nice body, which she'd had a brief—if somewhat embarrassing —chance to survey.

The man had three of the most rambunctious kids she'd seen in a long time. They reminded Brit of her own home on the farm and her rowdy family of six brothers and sisters. Suddenly she missed them and longed for those gone-forever days.

She hadn't seen any signs that Harrison had a wife. And little Avery had revealed that they were motherless. Was Harrison a widower? Regardless, Brit had her work cut out for her.

Snapping back to the reality of the enormous job she was facing, Brit picked up the phone and began dialing furiously. Eventually, she ran through every number in her staff book. With a heavy sigh she dialed one last, very familiar number.

"Riley? Please, you've got to help me tonight."

"Did your promotional gimmick work, Brit?"

Brit lowered her voice. "I've infiltrated the enemy

lines, and he needs me to arrange a dinner party for potential investors tonight, and—"

"Oh, no you don't! I won't be your cook again."

"No, no, Riley. This is easy. Phillipe is coming to cook. But Sir Wilfred can't make it, and—"

Riley's voice became immediately affected. "Your veddy proper English butler is indisposed? Tut-tut, Brit. It's your problem."

"Riley, please. Someone has to serve."

"How could you think of ruining my Saturday night like this? Watch my lips, Brit. *No.*"

"Fortunately I can't see your lips. Riley, you're my friend, aren't you?"

"Sort of."

"Sort of? Riley, please do this for me. If you really care about me and my future, you'll do it."

"Have you seen the robot yet?"

"Which one? He's got at least a dozen around here. I need you, Riley. Remember the time—"

She was interrupted by a loud groan on the telephone.

Brit hung up with a sigh. *Riley Dugan, you'd better get over here tonight and help me out of this mess.*

CHAPTER TWO

Brit stood in the middle of the Kent living room and surveyed her handiwork. There was no time to wash the handprints from windows or have the rug professionally shampooed. She was thankful that this was an evening event and that the sun would disappear any minute. With the lamps on low beam and with a judicious use of candles, she could disguise the scarred furniture and the stained upholstery.

The sound of rattling pots and French curses drifted from the kitchen. Phillipe didn't like rushed occasions; he declared they inhibited his creative spirit. And his initial reaction to the gadget-filled kitchen had been distrust. But now the delectable aromas wafting out to Brit assured her that Phillipe would provide a tempting gourmet dinner tonight. Despite his complaining, the retired chef loved the opportunity to cook for the Quintessential Woman.

The kids were ensconced in an upstairs bedroom with hamburgers and fries from their favorite fast-food spot. Harrison had moved both the television set and the video recorder upstairs, and Brit had rented every single Rocky movie available. Harrison was upstairs, too, changing into the black suit she'd had cleaned and pressed for him this afternoon.

When Brit hung the suit in Harrison's closet two hours before, vivid memories of their morning encounter, of his towel-draped masculine form, bombarded her. The spicy scent of his aftershave still lingered in the room, and his presence was everywhere, from the rumpled, unmade bed to his bathrobe thrown over a chair. She had hurried out of the room and closed the door.

Now he was dressing upstairs, buttoning his shirt across his broad chest, pulling his slacks on, zipping them. Brit shook her head in dismay. This had to stop. Of course he'd look devastating in the suit. He looked terrific with practically nothing on. So what? He was the enemy.

Brit consulted her watch. Everything was on schedule except for Riley Dugan. If Riley didn't show up to serve the meal, Brit would have to do it herself, and she wasn't appropriately dressed. But no one would be available to deal with the kids if the charms of movies and fast food wore off. Damn, Riley was already twenty minutes late!

"Sacré bleu!" Phillipe burst from the kitchen waving a spoon. "It pinched me!"

"What pinched you?"

"I pushed a button, an arm came out, and snap! Just so, on my derriere." He rubbed his generous backside and sniffed indignantly.

Brit tried not to laugh as she eyed the pudgy, gray-haired chef. "That's the Goody-Grabber."

"Phillipe is no goody!"

"The machine can't tell. I encountered that monster this afternoon and found out Mr. Kent had designed it for his daughter, Avery. The button releases the Goody-Grabber, and another lever moves the hand up and down so she can reach things and put them back. Avery's only this tall." Brit held her hand waist-high.

The chef scowled darkly. "That Goody-Grabber better stay away from Phillipe."

"I'll ask Mr. Kent if we can turn it off for the night," Brit said soothingly. "How are the Cornish hens coming along?"

"Ah!" Phillipe brightened. *"Magnifique!* In spite of that—that stove"—he lifted his eyes to the heavens—"and no time to properly prepare. But I will provide a superb meal as always."

"I'm sure you will. I know the stove is a little strange."

"And the sink and the refrigerator and the garbage disposal and—"

The roar of a motorcycle in the driveway interrupted his harangue.

"Yes, well, Mr. Kent enjoys his gadgets," Brit said over her shoulder as she hurried to the door. Riley must be here. Thank God.

"Humph." Phillipe turned and stomped back to the kitchen, grumbling as he went.

Brit opened the door with a sigh of relief that turned to a gasp of surprise. "Riley, what is that you have on? You don't intend to serve in that?"

"Mais oui!" Riley pranced into the room and twirled to reveal a mass of snowy white petticoats under her short black skirt. "I look *très bon, n'est-ce pas?"*

"Your French is terrible, Riley."

"But I got a B in college!"

"Look, I want someone who will blend into the woodwork, someone conservative like Sir Wilfred. Instead I get a French tart in fishnet stockings! You must have been a sight to see riding your motorcycle over here."

"I did turn a few heads, but I'm sure that fender-bender wasn't my fault."

"My God."

"People should pay attention to their driving, Brit!"

"Other people should be less of a distraction, Riley!"

"Listen, roomie, I gave up my Saturday night for you, and I intend to have a little fun if I have to work." She adjusted the tiny white cap that was perched on her black curls. "The costume agency said this is a typical French maid's outfit, and I think it suits me. Like my shoes?"

Brit glanced at the four-inch stiletto heels. "If you fall face first into the tomato and mozzarella gratin you're carrying, don't come crying to me."

"I won't fall. I sell these things, remember? Besides, if one of the women notices them, I thought I could slip her my card and—"

"Absolutely not. No soliciting for your own business tonight."

"But it would be such a great opportunity. These people have money and probably not a lot of time to shop for shoes, and I could—"

"No."

"Will you get their names at least? So I can call them next week?"

"I'll see what I can do. No promises. Goodness, Riley! I'm amazed you're not the president of General Motors by now, with your aggressive sales techniques."

"Fancy Footwork will be listed on the New York Stock Exchange someday. Mark my words."

"I believe you."

"So did you see the robot?"

"Not so loud, Riley," Brit said, clutching her roommate's arm and steering her toward the kitchen. "Harrison might come downstairs any minute."

"Oh, so it's 'Harrison' now? How does Mrs. Kent feel about that?"

"He's a widower, Riley, with three little kids."

"Oh. Ooh la la. Talk about a perfect infiltrating setup. Have you offered him a long-term contract so you can spy on that mechanical housekeeper he's building?"

"Not yet. I wanted to get through this dinner first. That's why it's so important that we do a good job. Come on. Phillipe will explain about each course, and you can help me set the table. They'll be here in half an hour."

"Brit?" A masculine voice caused them to turn around before they reached the kitchen. "The house looks great, and the kids are as happy as clams. I'm impressed."

"So am I," muttered Riley under her breath as she beamed at Harrison.

"I'm glad you're pleased," Brit said, staring in

31

frank appreciation at her employer. The white shirt emphasized his broad shoulders, and he'd chosen a pearl-gray sweater vest that called attention to his well-developed chest. Riley tugged surreptitiously at Brit's sleeve. "Uh, I'd like you to meet my roommate, Riley Dugan."

Harrison turned to her. "You work for Brit?"

Riley laughed and curtsied. *"Certainement, monsieur."*

"Riley's temporary," Brit explained, giving her roommate a dark look. "She agreed to fill in tonight when my regular butler couldn't make it."

"Riley?" Harrison smiled. "I figured it would be Bridget or Fifi."

"My mama, she is from Paris," Riley said in a curious combination of Italian and French accents.

Brit groaned. "Riley—"

"Excusez-moi. I must have—how you say?—pow-wow with Phillipe." Riley tottered into the kitchen like a windup toy on her impossibly high heels.

Harrison watched her go. "Are you sure she can walk in those things?"

"Don't worry, she'll be fine."

"Her French is terrible."

"She got a B in college."

Harrison rubbed his chin. "I'm beginning to wonder if I can afford this. A French chef and a French maid sound expensive."

"Not with the Quintessential Woman," Brit assured him with a trace of pride. "Riley won't charge any more than my regular butler, Sir Wilfred, and he's very reasonable."

"Sir Wilfred? You've got quite a cast of characters working for you."

Brit chuckled. "True. And most of them are over sixty-five."

"Retired folks?"

"Don't let them hear you use that word," Brit cautioned with a smile. "None of them are the retiring type. They're perfect for my business because their skills are excellent and yet they don't want a full-time position or full-time wages."

Harrison nodded approvingly. "Ingenious. Well, do I pass inspection?" He faced her, hands in the pockets of his black suit pants. "I'll put the jacket on later. I hate the damned things, but tonight's important. I have to look as if I have a business head."

Brit tried to appear dispassionate. "The gray and burgundy tie blends well, and the gray sweater vest is a nice touch." And she longed to do just that— touch. The soft material begged for a woman's caress.

"Did I get the gray one? I wasn't sure. I have a tan one, too, and I mix them up all the time."

"You're color-blind, aren't you?"

"Yep."

She leaned closer to examine the ebony eyes behind the frames of his aviator-style glasses.

"I don't think you can tell by looking, Brit."

"Oh!" She drew back immediately. "I didn't mean to stare. I've never known anyone who was color-blind."

"It's like watching black-and-white television instead of color, or so I'm told. I can imagine what

33

color looks like and wish I could see it. For example, your hair is probably blond or light red, but I don't know which."

"Blond."

"And your eyes fool me. They're sort of a blend of dark and light, and they change."

"They're blue-green, I guess. People tell me they get dark when I'm angry or—" She braked her sentence to a skidding halt.

"Or what?" A smile twitched the corners of his mouth as his gaze captured hers.

"Um, nothing."

"I may be color-blind, but I can tell you're blushing."

"I don't blush, Mr. Kent!"

"And now your eyes are getting dark. Does that mean you're angry? Or . . . ?" He lifted one eyebrow.

"Mr. Kent, I still have several things to do before your guests arrive." She turned away abruptly.

He caught her arm. "Hey, Brit, I was only teasing. Don't be offended."

She glanced back at him, and the gentle humor in his dark eyes made her smile in spite of herself. "Okay." His hand remained, lightly grasping, on her arm, and Brit felt herself drifting closer to him, swaying a little as something in his gaze beckoned softly.

"Dad! Murph the Smurf ate all the fries!" Shane bounded down the stairs. "Can I pop him one?"

Harrison wrenched his attention from Brit and turned to face his son. "No. He's smaller than you."

"Yeah, and because of it he gets away with murder."

Brit passed a trembling hand across her forehead. She was definitely drawn to Harrison Kent—the enemy. "Murph the Smurf?" she questioned, more to regain her equilibrium than because she really wanted to know about the nickname.

"I call him that because he's such a little half-pint, like those midget blue people on TV," Shane said. "But he's a real pest, too."

Brit put a hand on the boy's shoulder. "Come on, Shane. You know how important this dinner is to your father, and we can't very well have a french-fry war going on upstairs. If you'll forget this for now, I'll make sure your dessert helping is the biggest."

Shane grinned. "Sounds good. What is it, chocolate cake?"

"Apple snow."

"Oh." Some of his enthusiasm ebbed. "Never heard of that. What's in it?"

"Applesauce and meringue topped with a wonderful caramel sauce."

Shane looked doubtful. "Can I put chocolate sauce on it, too?"

"Not in front of Phillipe, if you value your life," Brit said, laughing. "But I'll smuggle some upstairs."

"Great! Well, I've gotta get back. We're ready to watch the next Rocky movie." Shane raced back up the stairs.

Harrison turned to her, admiration in his dark eyes. "Nicely handled, Brit."

She shrugged. "I grew up in a big family. Besides, the Quintessential Woman can do—"

"I know. Anything." He smiled.

Brit caught her breath at the warmth that surrounded her as she basked in that dazzling smile. She lifted her face, as if to the sun.

"You're really amazing. You've taken care of everything, Brit."

"It's all part of our service." She forced herself to focus on the job ahead instead of on the gorgeous man standing in front of her. "I plan to stay behind the scenes tonight as a coordinator, so don't worry about the kids or the food."

"I won't. I see how capable you are. But there is one thing. As I mentioned, tonight will include a demonstration of a small prototype of the robot. He'll be set up in the kitchen, ready to roll out when I turn on the remote control. I'd like him to serve dessert, in fact. Would you make sure nothing or nobody's in the way and he's ready to go?"

"Will he take up much room? Phillipe is already spooked about all the gadgets, and he might rebel at seeing another one installed in his kitchen."

"Don't worry. This little guy fits nicely into a corner. He's not even three feet tall, and besides, he's cute."

"I hope Phillipe thinks so."

"Phillipe won't even notice him. Will you help?"

"Okay." *What a chump I am,* Brit thought. Aiding and abetting the enemy. Even the dinner itself, which she had eagerly offered to make into a success for him, was paving the way for his robot to be financed. But unless she helped him now, she

36

wouldn't know what this mechanical monster was all about until it was too late. The fact that Harrison Kent had a million-dollar smile had nothing to do with her decision to cooperate. Nothing at all.

An hour later, cocktails were over and Riley was sweeping back and forth between the kitchen and the dining room with platters of food and bottles of Chardonnay. With every break in the action, she reported on the progress of the evening to Brit.

"In two instances the husband obviously rules the roost, and the men are completely in favor of this robot stuff," Riley concluded, setting down an empty dish ringed with the remains of tomato and mozzarella gratin. "But the third couple will be tough to convince. I gather it's the woman's money, and she's skeptical that a machine can be built to do all that Harrison claims."

"I hope she's right," Brit said in a low voice while uncorking another bottle of wine. "I'd like nothing better than for Mr. Harrison Kent's robotic house-keeper to be a failure."

"He's kind of cute, though."

"The robot?" Brit glanced at Harrison's small prototype, an R2D2 sort of creature sitting in a corner well out of Phillipe's way.

"No. Harrison. Unfortunately he's not my type, but I think he might be yours."

"What a silly idea!" Brit darted a look at the French chef, whose head was cocked in their direction while he intently stirred the caramel sauce for dessert. "Are you listening, Phillipe?"

"Certainly not."

"Well, don't. Riley's talking nonsense."

The gray-haired man glanced up. "He's not right for you, *chérie*. Too many gadgets in this house."

Riley smiled and started out the door. "Yes, but consider that a man who makes so many gadgets is probably creative in . . . other ways." With a chuckle she disappeared before Brit could utter an indignant response.

"Where's the dessert?" Shane poked his head into the kitchen.

"Any minute now, Shane. Stick around and you can take it up."

"Avery's about to zonk out."

"It is getting pretty late. Phillipe, is the sauce ready?"

"Do not be impatient." The chef lifted the spoon and watched the caramel liquid drip from it. "Ah. Perfection."

Shane gave an exaggerated wink. "Brit, while you're next to the refrigerator, would you get out the you-know-what?"

At that moment Riley breezed back into the kitchen carrying empty plates, and Shane's mouth dropped open as he followed her teetering walk across to the dishwasher.

Brit caught his look of wonder and smiled to herself. Boys will be boys. "Shane, this is Riley Dugan."

Riley turned and gave the boy a brilliant smile. "Hello, Shane."

He closed his mouth abruptly. "Glad to meet you."

"Same here." Riley glanced at Brit. "They're moving into the living room for dessert. Harrison

38

has the remote control, and he said you knew what to do."

"That's right."

"Okay. I'll clear the rest of the dishes, then."

"Don't walk in front of that robot, Riley. You're liable to get bowled over."

Riley laughed. "He's not my type either, Brit." She ruffled Shane's hair. "I like this kind."

Shane turned beet red and stared after her with rapt attention until she was out of sight. "Brit, do you think maybe she could, uh—that is, maybe, uh, bring our dessert up?"

"You can carry your own dessert, Shane," Brit said firmly.

He sighed in resignation. "Okay." He glanced at the robot as a little light on top of it flashed on. "So Dad's gonna run the little guy around?"

"He wants it to serve dessert. I didn't know he'd be ready so soon, but I guess we can start with coffee while Phillipe finishes dishing out the apple snow."

"Yeah, Dad loves doing this," Shane said, nodding. "I'll get the tray that goes on the little guy's arms." He pulled the tray from a cupboard and squatted down next to the humming machine. "I wonder why Dad hasn't raised his arms?" He studied the robot more closely. "Uh-oh. They're jerking but not going up. The arms are stuck."

"Stuck?" Brit walked over and bent down to look. "Can you do something?"

"I dunno." Shane squinted at the arms. "Maybe this bolt is on too tight, but we don't have a wrench."

Brit thought quickly. "We have serving tongs." She jumped up and found the metal tongs in a drawer.

"Might work." Shane closed the tongs around the nut and twisted. The nut budged a fraction, and the robot's arms shot up. "It did!" He grinned at Brit. "We fixed it."

She smiled back. "We sure did. Now quick, load the tray and the coffee cups onto him."

As the little robot rolled out the door bearing its tray of cups and saucers, Shane and Brit stood side by side and watched in delight. Then Shane stuck out his hand, palm up. "Gimme five."

Brit slapped his palm and laughed, then turned her own hand up, and he repeated the gesture. She admitted to herself to having had a wonderful time and also to being as crazy as a bedbug. If she hadn't helped Shane fix the robot, Harrison's investors might have been disillusioned about his abilities and perhaps they would have refused to finance his project. What was wrong with her sense of self-preservation?

Much later, after Phillipe had left, Brit stood alone in the kitchen unloading the dishwasher and asked herself the same question. Riley had also left, but Brit didn't need her reports to know the evening had been a success. The departing guests sounded far too jovial to have reservations about their financial investment.

Harrison would have the money he needed for the domestic robot largely because of her. She should have found some way to sabotage him tonight. Hell, the opportunity had been right there, and she had jumped in like a Girl Scout and saved the day! Typical. A crisis presented itself, and she always came to the rescue.

"Hallelujah, let's celebrate!" Harrison burst into the kitchen and grabbed her by the shoulders. "They pledged the money!" he chortled, spinning her around. "Hey, I've got some champagne in the refrigerator. Let's drink to our success."

Releasing Brit as quickly as he'd grabbed her, Harrison jerked open the refrigerator door and rummaged around until he found the bottle. Then he plugged a gadget Brit hadn't noticed before into a wall socket and stuck the bottle into it. In the space of two seconds the cork flew into the center of the room.

"What was that?" she asked in surprise.

"The Cork-Torque. Didn't you use it for the wine tonight?"

Brit shook her head. She wouldn't have dared. She imagined what would have happened if the Cork-Torque had flung debris into Phillipe's spinach soufflé or caramel sauce.

Harrison poured two glasses full and handed one to Brit. "To the multidigital latitudinarian scope robot."

Brit stared at him and bemusedly raised her glass. What was she doing, drinking a toast to her nemesis? But she did it. "To the multidigital whatsis."

Harrison laughed and drank his champagne. "I'll come up with a better name. Or the kids will. Where are they, by the way?"

"Sound asleep."

"You got them to bed? You're amazing." He saluted her with his glass and took another generous swallow. "This is one of the best nights of my life. The investors liked my prospectus, Brit! The schematic convinced them that I knew what I was doing, and when the little guy came in, the deal was sewn up."

His enthusiasm was contagious, and Brit smiled. "I'm happy for you." Strangely, she was telling the truth.

He set down his glass and paced back and forth in front of her. "I've done a lot of the preliminary construction, of course. With a little luck, the final phase won't take long. Brit, this is what I've dreamed of for years. And now I have the money. It's just fantastic!" Without warning he grabbed her again and waltzed her around the kitchen.

"We did it, we did it," he chanted, then kissed her firmly on the mouth.

She went rigid with shock. His exuberant expression faded as he registered the dazed look on her face. He dropped his arms.

"Guess I got carried away there," he mumbled, massaging the back of his neck nervously. He glanced at her and smiled self-consciously. "You probably don't care all that much whether this deal came through or not."

"Oh, no, I—" She touched her mouth with the tips of her fingers. She'd certainly been kissed before, and with a lot more finesse than Harrison just displayed. So why was her body reacting with such alacrity to that one quick, careless pressure of his lips?

"I needed to share my excitement with someone

and you were handy," he said with an apologetic shrug.

She wanted to deck him. Handy? And she'd thought he meant something by the gesture. He was only ridding himself of pent-up emotion by using the nearest human being.

"As long as we're discussing how handy I am," she said with tight control, "I have a special offer from the Quintessential Woman. For this month only, we'll clean your house twice weekly for half price. Are you interested?"

"Cleaning?" He looked confused. "Oh, that's right. That's how this all got started. I sort of forgot."

"Well?" She crossed her arms. Once his signature was on the dotted line, she'd get the hell out of there.

"Uh, sure. Sounds like a good idea." He smiled sheepishly. "We could use some cleaning up, I guess." He paused and glanced at her. "You'll assign one of your retirees to the job, I suppose."

"As a matter of fact, I'll handle the job personally. This is a special promotion, and we need all our staff—including me."

"That will be nice," he said, looking directly into her eyes.

Brit felt the magnetic pull of his gaze, and she swallowed hard. The enemy. She had to remember exactly who this man was.

CHAPTER THREE

"You're spending the night with Harrison Kent? I'm impressed. You didn't mess around with dates —just went right for the long-term contract!"

"Not exactly *with* him, Riley," Brit said, neatly folding her skimpy bikini panties into the small suitcase on her bed. "This is for the short term. Harrison's going out of town for a few days. I'm just staying with the kids and taking care of the household while he's gone. Actually, this is a normal progression of events—just an extension of my complete services. Good for business."

"Good for your spy network, you mean," Riley said with a twinkle in her eyes.

Brit cast her roommate a quick look and changed the subject. "I've lasted longer than most with the Kent family. Two weeks seems to be the limit."

"Ah, but you have an ulterior motive, Brit. I think it's exciting! You say he won't be home?"

Brit shook her head and continued to pack. "It'll just be me and the three kids."

Riley swept her arm dramatically. "Just you and the ultimate robot. Plus the mad scientist's hundred-and-one oddball gadgets that creep up behind you and pinch. You'd better watch out, Brit. There may be a spy in the bunch!" She paused and laughingly considered the possibility. "A spy spying on the spy!"

"You're crazy, Riley." But Brit couldn't help laughing, too. "All they do is bounce up and down the halls, picking cobwebs out of corners."

"I wish we had one that would do that. Maybe you could borrow a robot for a while?"

Brit shot her a hard glance. "Sounds like treason to me, Riley. Anyway, they're not perfect. Bumpy knocks into everything as he vacuums the floor."

"Good grief, Brit. You're even calling them by name, as if they were real or something."

"You know, when you work around them for a while, they start to seem almost human." Brit studied two sweaters, then decided to take them both.

"I tell you, Brit, it's a weird household with all those robots running around. Like a bunch of humanoids."

"You should talk about weird households, Riley." Brit motioned to the stacks of shoeboxes surrounding her dark-haired friend. "And even though Harrison may be involved in strange creations, his children are just kids. Average, busy, intelligent."

"And superactive!"

"It does take lots of energy and creativity to keep them out of trouble. But they're neat kids. That's one reason Harrison invented so many gadgets. They help him keep an eye on the kids as well as eliminate wasted time and motion."

"Sounds like you have more than a passing interest in this particular client and his family, Brit."

45

"It's strictly business," Brit replied.

"Do I detect a touch of regret in your tone?"

"Harrison's far too busy to notice—uh, to be concerned about—anything but his project. It occupies every active moment of his days."

"What about those lonely moments of his nights?"

"Oh, Riley, I don't know what he does during off-hours. Ours is a professional relationship."

"How dull."

"But he needs assistance to maintain order and consistency in that rambunctious household of his. Someone efficient and trustworthy. That's why he hired me."

"Trustworthy?" Riley hooted with laughter. "Little does he know you're really a spy. What's the superrobot like?"

"I, uh, haven't seen it."

"Why not? What have you been doing over there all this time? Just baby-sitting?"

Brit hedged. "Well, I haven't really had a chance."

"Now you will! You'll have complete freedom this weekend to slip in there and inspect away. Maybe even to pull a few wires and foul up the works. Good planning, Brit." Riley rubbed her hands together gleefully.

Brit gazed doubtfully across the room. "I don't know. He, uh, trusts me, Riley. He hired me to take care of his entire household—even his children. How could I break that trust?"

"Guilty conscience, huh? So how the heck do you

expect to find out about this humanoid that has the potential to destroy your hard-earned business?"

"I'd like for Harrison to trust me enough to tell me about it. Or maybe he'll show it to me."

"Then what?" Riley puzzled.

"I don't know. Maybe we could work something out. Maybe it isn't as bad as I think."

"Boy, are you optimistic." Riley rolled her eyes. "Is this the same person who talked about 'search and destroy' only a few weeks ago?"

"Right now I just want to understand the enemy's strengths. It would be nice if he'd volunteer to show me—"

"Show you his etchings?" Riley interrupted gleefully. "I can see it now! Come on into my *labora*tory, Ms. McIver. I want to show you my, uh, thingamagig."

Brit rolled her eyes. "Well, he might, you know. But first he has to notice me, then maybe we—"

"Wait a minute. I think I'm getting the picture now." Riley sobered quickly. "You want him to notice you? Why don't you spice up your wardrobe a little and catch his attention? I'll bet these would do the trick!" She grabbed a pair of purple polka-dot spike heels and thrust them forward.

"Yes, especially if I fell down the stairs and broke my neck." Brit shrugged the suggestion away.

"Try them. They're just your size. My client changed her mind and decided to return them."

"I can understand why," Brit said, grabbing her tennis shoes from the closet. "They're outrageous."

"You're impossible, Brit." Riley ran her hands through her unruly hair and turned back to her task. "I wish Harrison'd invent a robot to help me eliminate *this* waste of time and motion. I'll never get all these stupid figures straight. And this darned column of numbers just won't add up." She chewed her pencil and started punching the small calculator with a vengeance.

Brit shook her head. "I'm not sure if a robot could help, Riley. You'd need a CPA to straighten out this mess. Someone with a brain like a calculator and the patience of a saint." She chose two pairs of slacks from her closet, one gray and the other brown.

"Looks hopeless to me," Riley moaned.

Brit glanced over at the uneven stacks of shoeboxes that characterized Riley's side of the long, narrow bedroom, and also served as the storage area for her shoe business. It pointed up the extreme differences between the two friends. Riley's side of the room consisted of a single unmade bed, a cluttered dresser, a thriving four-foot-high potted palm, a huge asparagus fern hanging in the corner, and fifty-odd shoeboxes waiting to be delivered or returned to the factory.

On the other hand, Brit's area was defined by neatness, almost as if someone had drawn a chalk mark down the center of the room. Her bed was made, her bookshelf was organized, and her dresser was shiny and swept clear of clutter. A small desk held the schedule book and other paraphernalia of her business.

The two had been friends for a long time and shared similar goals. Because Riley's enthusiasm complemented Brit's sense of order, their existence seldom lacked excitement and fun.

"I can't think of anything more dull and boring than to endure the weekend alone trying to balance my books"—Riley moaned—"while you're spending an exciting weekend in the home of the handsome, eccentric inventor, Harrison Kent."

"What happened to the mad scientist?"

Riley ignored Brit's dig. "Personally, I was hoping you'd need a partner to break into his workshop on your search and destroy mission of that electronic monster he's supposed to be building."

"Thanks. I'll keep your offer in mind," Brit murmured. "But don't plan on it."

"Heck, Brit. Just looking at the crazy thing won't defy his trust. I'd like to see it. Aren't you curious—just a little bit?"

Brit ignored the question. "If I spy on Harrison, I'll never gain his trust." She sat on the edge of the bed and pulled on her tennis shoes.

"But you'd get his attention, I'll bet. What you need is . . ." Riley paused to assess Brit's attire. "You're wearing that?"

"Sure, why not?" Brit looked down at her basic beige sweater and matching slacks. "These are good working clothes."

"Um-hm. If you're trying to catch Harrison's eye, that's not the way. Get rid of these drab rags. You need a little pizzazz in your wardrobe, Brit." Riley shoved aside her calculator and dove into Brit's closet. "How about this dynamite combination?" She whipped out a red blouse and a yellow vest. "He'll have to notice you in this. You look smashing in red, with that blond hair. Catch his eye first, then his mind." Riley started rummaging in her boxes.

"Don't bother, Riley. Wild colors won't catch Harrison's eye—he's color-blind."

"Ah." Riley reconsidered for a moment. "Then what you need is to give him some zingy shapes. Show a little skin."

"What?"

"Oh, I mean, show off your shapely legs. Wear a skirt, and make sure it's short enough. I think I have the perfect sweater somewhere. Yes! Here it is!" Riley pulled a daring item from one of her drawers. "This one has a deep V-neck in the back. And it's purple to match the polka-dot shoes. Wonderful!"

"Riley, I can't wear something like this to clean the house and watch the kids."

"Why not?"

"Well, it looks dumb, that's why."

"Trust me, Brit. Take this skirt, this sweater, and these pumps. Wear them the day he comes back from his business trip. Believe me, he'll notice. And just see if there aren't some positive results."

"But, Riley, not the purple polka dots!"

"Come on, Brit. These will make your legs look mahvelous, dahling. Take my word for it."

Brit sighed. "Okay, okay. Give them to me." She stuffed the wild shoes into a side pocket of her suitcase. Maybe Riley was right. It was time to see if the inventor had an eye for shape if not color.

"You have to take advantage of your opportunities while you have them," Riley encouraged. "And while you have a job there."

"You make it sound as if my days in the Kent household were numbered. I plan to stay until the robot's finished."

"You never know. Didn't you say most don't make it over two weeks?"

Brit sighed and picked up her suitcase. "Okay, I'll give it a whirl. But don't be disappointed if he just looks right through me like he always does. Anyway, he has three kids who desperately need his attention."

Riley grinned confidently. "Mark my words, Brit. You will get his undivided attention when he sees you in that outfit. And don't forget to smile."

"How's this?" Brit forced her lips into an upward curve.

"Poifect!"

"Do me a favor, Riley. Finish your darned inventory this weekend. You're getting impossible, always thinking up diversions to keep you from your spreadsheets. How are you going to make it to the New York Stock Exchange if you can't even balance your books?"

Riley flopped back onto her bed. "Sounds like a boring weekend!"

"Make sure to record all my calls and messages." Brit paused by the door. "I'm not sure if I should thank you for your wardrobe advice and these godawful shoes. Something tells me to be cautious."

"Be grateful. They're going to make a big splash!"

"Why does that phrase send chills down my back?" Brit waved and fled down the stairs before Riley had time to drag out any more wild clothes for enticing Harrison Kent. Secretly, though, she

51

thought it might be fun. And she couldn't wait to see his reaction to her polka-dot shoes.

Harrison loosened his basic brown tie and settled behind the wheel of his dull green Volvo. Pulling into the airport traffic, he jerked the tie completely off and freed the top two buttons of his white shirt. His presentation in New York had gone without a hitch and had been well-received by his colleagues. Undoubtedly it would propel his career. He should be elated over the business aspects, yet all he could think of was getting back home.

Home to the kids. And . . . to Brit. Well, he couldn't expect the kids to share his personal elation over the business, but Brit might understand. Even now he could see her bright, enthusiastic smile. Damn it, he wanted to see her.

Oh, he knew the kids were fine. He'd talked to them daily. And all they could say was "Brit did this with us" and "Brit took us there."

The lady was amazing. So well-organized. So thorough. So pretty.

Thoughts of the kids were completely abandoned as Harrison became preoccupied with Brit. Her image floated beside him in the car as he battled the traffic from Dulles Airport. He smiled as he thought of her, breezing into his life like a little whirlwind, taking charge, doing an excellent job, always cheerful. He should let her know how much he appreciated her work, how he had quickly come to depend on her. Maybe he should do something extra, like give her a bonus.

Hell, maybe he should take her out to dinner and

get to know her better. Yes, that was it! They needed to be alone.

Just the two of them, with no interruptions from kids. Getting to know each other better . . . looking into each other's eyes . . . holding hands. Suddenly, he could hardly wait to see her, to touch her lovely face. Her skin looked like smooth silk—so enticing. The rest of her, what little he'd seen, was slender and attractive. His foot pressed the accelerator, and the Volvo shot forward. White shoulders, full breasts, small waist, slim hips. Mentally he saw her nude, and—

Damn! Missed the Vienna exit! Harrison's palms were sweaty when he took the next ramp and circled back home. How long had it been since his palms had been sweaty over a woman? He turned into his driveway, and Avery bounded out to greet him.

Happily he swung her up in his arms. "How's my little pepper? Have I missed you!"

Avery squeezed his neck, then launched into a breathless avalanche. "Daddy, Daddy! Shane's gone to the hospital, and Murphy went along, and they made me stay with Mrs. Weeples from across the street, and I'm mad 'cause I'm missing all the fun of seeing them put a cast on his arm!"

Harrison rocked back on his heels. "Whose arm?"

"Shane's, 'cause he broke it."

"Broke it? How? Is he hurt bad? Where's Brit?"

"That's what I'm mad about, Daddy. I'm trying to tell you, Brit took Shane to the hospital. Murph got to go along and I didn't."

53

Harrison grabbed his briefcase. "I think we'd better get to the bottom of this. Is Mrs. Weeples inside?"

He listened as his neighbor explained the details of the bike accident that had broken Shane's arm just a couple of hours ago. "Rest assured, Mr. Kent. That young lady you hired to take care of the children is certainly efficient. She watched them like a hawk this entire weekend, but Shane just managed to slip away. It was purely an accident—not her fault at all."

"Where did it happen?" Harrison asked.

"Right down the road. I saw the whole thing myself. That son of yours is a little too daring for his own good. He skidded in some loose gravel. Lucky there were no cars coming. You could tell right away his arm was broken, but that young lady was so calm and reassuring. She took immediate command of the situation. Made a sling from a dish towel and called me. She knew just what to do."

Avery tugged on her father's sleeve. "You should see Brit, Daddy. She has on some new purple shoes. Neat!"

Harrison ignored his little daughter and turned back to Mrs. Weeples. "Is Shane hurt badly? Anything else besides the broken arm?"

"Just a few scrapes here and there."

Avery stomped over and switched the TV channel. "I had to miss all the fun."

Harrison thanked Mrs. Weeples, and she left somewhat reluctantly. Obviously she, like Avery, didn't want to miss the excitement, either. Before

54

long, Brit returned with the injured Shane and his brother.

Harrison patiently listened to the details of the accident and the process of applying the cast. Finally he ushered the three rowdy children upstairs. Then he turned to Brit. "I understand you reacted calmly in the face of crisis—again. You're to be commended, Brit."

"I'm terribly sorry about the accident, Harrison. I shouldn't have let him get out of my sight."

Harrison held his hand up to hush her. "Brit, I don't hold you responsible. Shane has always been accident-prone. And Mrs. Weeples is right. Sometimes he's too daring for his own good."

Brit took a deep breath and faced Harrison. "Actually, Shane slipped out without my knowledge. And I gave them all strict instructions about that."

"Slipped out?" Harrison's dark brows rose. "Then he disobeyed. Do you think he should be punished, Brit?"

"Well, I don't know about punishing." She swallowed hard. "I don't think Shane did anything intentionally. He's been punished quite severely with this broken arm."

Harrison pursed his lips. "Okay, I'll have a serious talk with him. We'll let it ride this time, but next time he disobeys you, he'll be grounded."

"Disobeys me? You mean there'll be a next time? I can keep my job?"

"Of course."

"But I feel so helpless." She gestured. "And responsible."

"Don't." He moved closer, and taking her hand,

55

sandwiched it between his. "You did your job as adequately as you could. Children are not foolproof. Now, don't feel bad about this, Brit. It was an accident."

Warmth spread throughout her body as he took her hand, and she found herself wishing she could kiss his lips again, to feel their strength against hers. An overwhelming magnetism drew her to the man she had proclaimed to be her enemy. Right now, though, he was far from being her enemy. "That's a generous attitude, Harrison."

"I've been thinking about it, Brit, and I haven't been generous enough with you. Haven't told you how much I value your assets. Oh, hell, that sounds terribly chauvinistic. I mean your, uh, abilities."

She smiled at his quick recovery and noticed his very masculine assets. His skin was tanned against his white shirt, and a sprinkling of dark hair dared to curl through the open neck. The sight was somewhat unnerving, and she forced her eyes to meet his. "Thanks, Harrison. The last thing I expected today was a compliment from you."

"Oh? Why?"

"I thought you'd be furious about what happened with Shane. I do feel terrible about it."

He chuckled. "I'm human, Brit. I understand. Actually, I'd like to give you more than a compliment. You have my gratitude. Let me take you to dinner tomorrow night, and we'll discuss a raise."

Brit's head whirled. "A raise?" Her heart pounded wildly. Dinner? She wasn't sure if his touch or his words were sending her into orbit, but she was rapidly losing control.

"I think you deserve it. We'll go someplace nice. This episode today was above and beyond the call of duty."

"But, Harrison—"

"Can you make it tomorrow night?"

"Sure." She wondered if he could hear her heart thrumming.

"Good. How was your weekend, except for Shane's accident?" He continued to hold her hand, and she felt his strength and the precision of his fingers as they faintly caressed hers.

"My weekend?" she murmured weakly. She was breathless and flushed as she tried to concentrate on a reasonable answer. "No problems. Your phone messages are on your desk."

He nodded and continued to gaze at her for a moment longer. "You're very efficient, Brit."

She noted the way the light shaded his angular face. Suddenly she longed to touch his beard-roughened jaw. "Uh, how was your weekend, Harrison?"

"Thought you'd never ask." He grinned spontaneously like a little boy with good news. "I didn't trip getting up to the podium or forget the name of my research paper. My presentation went very well, but I'll admit I'm glad to get back home."

"Of course you are. The kids missed you."

"Oh, I doubt that. You kept them pretty busy. They think you're super, Brit."

"It's mutual. They're neat kids."

"They can tell you like them. And I, uh, I missed . . ." He paused as if unsure for a moment. "Missed you, Brit."

"M-me?"

"Yeah. I found myself looking forward to seeing you here. I was disappointed when you didn't open this door. Mrs. Weeples just doesn't do as a substitute."

Brit's mind went completely blank. What was he saying? How should she answer? "I hope my work has been satisfactory, Harrison."

"More than satisfactory, Brit. You're really handy to have around."

She stiffened and tugged her hand free. Handy? Oh, dear God, here she was lost in the depths of his dark, sensuous eyes and dreaming what it would be like to kiss those lips thoroughly. And he was talking "handy"! "I—thank you. I'd better be going, Harrison."

"I'll pick you up at seven tomorrow night."

She nodded and backed one step away.

"Are the polka dots on your shoes really purple?"

Gasping, Brit thought of her feet for the first time in hours and looked down. "Y-yes," she mumbled. "How did you know?"

"Avery told me."

"Oh, yes. She liked them. Maybe I'll leave them for her to play dress-up. They really aren't my style."

"They're certainly bold."

"Yes, you're right. Too bold." She took another backward step before whirling away.

"Brit?"

"Yes?" She turned back around to face him.

"I didn't say they were too bold. Actually, I like them. They're different. And I like that sweater. Purple, too?"

58

Laughing nervously, she nodded. "Yes, it is."

"I'll bet you look pretty in that color."

She pushed her hair behind one ear and said clearly, "I'll leave my address on your desk in the study. And my phone number in case you change your mind."

"Not a chance," he said, smiling. "See you tomorrow night, Brit. We're going out on the town."

Harrison watched her disappear. Like a zombie, he stood in the middle of the family room thinking about Brit and what color her eyes were, and suddenly he hated the fact that he was color-blind.

Riley met her at the door. "How was your weekend?"

"Interesting. Hectic. Exciting. Wonderful. Scary." Brit trudged into the bedroom and dumped her suitcase in the corner.

"Scary? Why? Did the robots run amok?"

"No, the kids did!" Brit flopped spread-eagle onto her bed and mumbled, "Murphy did another experiment that spilled water all over the bathroom floor. I discovered that when they're home all the time, they eat all the time. And Shane broke his arm."

"Oh, my God! Is he okay?"

"Yep. Has a cast. Actually, at eleven it's a status symbol."

"Well, did the shoes work?"

Brit smiled broadly. "I guess so. We're having dinner tomorrow night. Just the two of us."

"Outrageous!" Riley bounced excitedly as she sat cross-legged in the middle of her bed. "Well, tell me all about it."

"There isn't much to tell. He asked me out, mentioned a bonus. And I said yes. Still strictly business, Riley. He thinks I'm handy to have around."

"He's going to find that you're not only handy, you're gorgeous! He liked that outfit, huh?"

Brit smiled devilishly. "He noticed me. And he said he's taking me someplace special."

"Mission accomplished!" Riley crowed. "Okay! We have twenty-four hours to figure out your next spectacular outfit. Let me see, now." Riley began sorting through Brit's closet. "What about this silver lamé?"

"Hm. I don't know. Think he can see the sparkle in the silver threads?"

"Of course he can see the sparkle! And just wait till he gets an eyeful of your curves wrapped in this, Brit. Plus, it has tactile appeal! He can feel, can't he?"

Brit nodded, smiling and remembering. "Yes, he can feel."

CHAPTER FOUR

Harrison stepped from the elevator and consulted the slip of paper in his hand. Apartment four twenty-two. He headed down the carpeted hall toward her door. His palms were sweating—again. He'd looked forward to this evening all day, and even working on the robot hadn't distracted him from thoughts of Brit. Tonight she'd be his alone, without the kids or the house to interfere. He punched the bell and shoved the slip of paper into his pocket.

When the door opened, he blinked in amazement.

"Hello, Harrison. Would you like to come in?" Brit smiled and stood aside for him to enter.

"Yes, I—yes! That dress . . ." He couldn't take his gaze from her. The shimmery material defined the sensuous curves of her body, and as she walked the cloth twinkled in response, taunting him to reach out and stroke the line of her hip, the swell of her breast.

"I hope it's not too—"

"Not too anything. Wow, Brit!" Her dress, in combination with an upswept hairstyle and a heady perfume, provided a powerful aphrodisiac that could easily drive him crazy before the night ended. Harrison longed to grab her, to feel the shimmery material give way beneath his grip, to—wait a minute, he had to slow down. "The dress is gorgeous," he said, congratulating himself on keeping his hands to himself when inside he was a raging savage. "What color is it?"

"Silver. Pretty much as you see it, I guess. I'll get my coat and purse."

Harrison leaned one shoulder against the wall in feigned nonchalance and watched her walk into the bedroom. "Did you do that for me? Wear something even a color-blind man could appreciate?" A blind man could appreciate that outfit, he decided, as long as the blind man was allowed unlimited exploration with his sense of touch.

"Riley picked this out," she called from the bedroom.

"Oh." Some of his excitement faded. He wished Brit had chosen the dress. Then he'd know exactly where they stood. "Thank Riley for me. Is she here?"

"No." Brit emerged carrying a white furry jacket and a small beaded purse. "Riley had a business dinner tonight, too."

His eyes narrowed. Were they playing games here? "What do you mean by *too?*"

Brit shrugged, and the cloth sparkled across her breasts. "Well, you are my employer, and you're taking me out because I've done a good job. That's business, isn't it?"

He looked into her eyes, trying to unravel the various signals she was sending. She'd worn a seductive dress but blamed the choice on her roommate. Still, there was her hair, pinned up in a slightly tousled, come-hither style that revealed the nape of her neck. Glittering earrings drew his attention to the soft skin of each earlobe. And the perfume—she'd never worn that fragrance to the house. He was sure of it. "Is that the way you want it, Brit? Strictly business?"

She paused, her expression wary. "I'm not sure."

"Aren't you?" He took a deep breath and crossed to her. "Maybe before the evening's over we can settle the issue."

"Maybe."

"Let me help you on with that." He took the jacket and held it for her. As she turned to slip her arms into the sleeves, the disconcerting magic of her perfume wafted upward, and Harrison fought the urge to bend his head and trail a kiss down the slender column of her neck.

The light jacket whispered over her shoulders. As he adjusted the soft fur around her, the tips of his fingers grazed her collarbone and lingered there for a moment longer than necessary. The courtesy was accomplished, but somehow he couldn't let her go. Not yet. He moved his hands to her shoulders and guided her around until she was facing him.

"I've never really considered you an employee, Brit," he said, watching her eyes, gauging her reaction to him.

"You . . . you haven't?" Her heartbeat thundered in her ears as his fingers buried themselves in the white fur and pulled her closer.

Behind the silver rim of his glasses his ebony eyes

were intent. "No." His gaze softened and swept her face before focusing on her parted lips. "And I've never had a business dinner that began like this."

As his mouth covered hers, Brit felt the same jolt as the first time they'd kissed, as if he were charged with a kind of electricity that brought pleasure instead of pain. Her eyelids fluttered closed as she concentrated on the feel of his mouth that fit hers so naturally, so perfectly.

When his lips parted, hers yielded automatically, and her breath quickened in time with his. His chin was rough, and the gentle abrasion stirred a primitive feminine instinct, a celebration of the differences between them.

She welcomed the thrust of his tongue as her senses whirled in a strangely familiar turmoil. When his hand slipped inside her coat and rubbed the small of her back, his touch created a clamoring warmth that demanded more, much more. Harrison gradually drew her forward until they were pressed together, moving gently, each learning the other's contours. Her hands found their way inside his dinner jacket. As they slid up his back, his muscles flexed under her gentle massage.

When his palm skimmed up her ribcage, Brit held her breath, knowing that if his caress became more intimate, she should stop him. But oh, God, she didn't want to. Her nipples grew taut, and she moaned deep in her throat as his hand brushed gently along the side of her breast. She could feel him tremble—or was it her own body quivering?

With a groan, he released her. Stepping back, he took a steadying breath. "Brit, I really didn't intend to—" He stopped and chuckled hoarsely. "Seems you've fogged up my glasses," he said, taking them off.

She shook her head, trying to clear the haze of desire from her eyes. "Mine, too, and I don't even wear any."

He laughed softly and took out a handkerchief. "That's nice to hear."

"Harrison, I don't want you to think that I'm in the habit of"—Brit gestured futilely—"of behaving like that. I'm not sure what came over me."

He smiled as he polished his glasses. "I'd like to think it had something to do with my irresistible charm. Besides, I'm glad to know you're not cool and collected all the time."

"Apparently I'm not."

"No." He winked. "Fortunately you're very human." He put the glasses back on. "That's better. Now I won't run us into a tree on the way to dinner."

"Wait." Brit stepped forward and took the handkerchief from him. "You've got a little lipstick . . ." She reached up and dabbed at his mouth.

He sighed and captured her hand. "Better let me do that. I'm only human, too." He wiped his mouth and stuffed the handkerchief back into his pocket.

"I need a little repair myself. Excuse me."

"Brit."

She paused and looked back at him. God, he was appealing, all in black, except for the snowy white dress shirt. She'd told him black was a power color, but she hadn't mentioned that it was also as sexy as hell.

"Stroke my ego a little, Brit. Tell me you had something to do with the decision on that dress."

"A little," she admitted. "I figured since color didn't matter, sparkle might."

"Let me tell you, sparkle matters," he said fervently.

Brit fought the urge to run back and fling herself into his arms. With an effort she turned away and escaped into the bedroom, determined not to let her emotions overwhelm her again. Her reaction to Harrison was far stronger than she had supposed it would be, and she needed time to sort out her feelings.

When she returned, lipstick in place, she smiled brightly. "Ready."

"Then, let's go." He tucked her arm through his as they walked out the door of the apartment.

On the ride down in the elevator Harrison continued to study her.

"You're making me nervous," she said at last.

"It's just such a contrast from your regular work clothes."

"That's what Riley wanted."

"Oh?" He guided her out of the elevator as it clunked to a stop. "And what did Brit want?"

"Brit wanted you to think she looked pretty."

"Will beautiful do?"

She smiled. "Yes."

"Say that word again."

"Yes."

"What a terrific word. Don't forget how to say it, Brit."

Her stomach fluttered with anticipation as he

helped her into the car. After their heated embrace she had no doubt what Harrison meant by his remark. Riley's plan was working with a vengeance.

The trouble was, it was working mutually, too. If Harrison was noticing Brit as a woman, she was also becoming extremely aware of him as a man. A virile, passionate man, capable of arousing long-buried emotions in her. She mustn't forget what had brought her to Harrison's house in the first place. Desire mustn't obstruct her mission to learn about the ominous domestic robot that might someday put her out of business.

But sitting across a candlelit dinner table from Harrison, Brit had trouble keeping her priorities straight. Light from the candle flame danced in his dark hair and flickered in his ebony eyes. He seemed far too handsome to be a computer genius, one whose brilliant invention could someday cause her financial ruin.

Although Brit made her living helping others plan menus, she now paid little attention to the elaborate food that had been placed before her. Her sense of taste and smell recorded the meal as delicious, but she was so engrossed in her dinner companion that she would not have been able to name what she ate.

Harrison told her of his years of unrewarding work for a major computer company. Slowly he described how, ironically, his wife Pam's life insurance policy had helped him escape the corporate world and become a self-employed inventor.

Brit wasn't quite sure how to handle a discussion

67

of Pam. "What a sad way to get something you wanted," she said hesitantly.

"Yes, it was." His expression was wistful but not tragic. "Still, I know Pam would have wanted me to do something positive with the money." His voice was firm, as if he'd come to terms with his loss.

"I'm sure you're right," Brit agreed, relieved that Harrison didn't seem consumed with grief. "And now you can build your dream—the ultimate domestic robot."

"Looks like I can."

Struggling to be true to her original purpose, Brit forced herself to ask another question about the machine that might someday put her out of business. "What will the robot be like, exactly?"

He grinned. "That sounds like a polite question a woman's supposed to ask her date. I'm sure you don't want to hear all the boring details."

"Maybe I do." *You'd be amazed at how interested I am,* she thought.

"No, I'd rather hear about you. I've monopolized the conversation enough."

"There's not much to tell," Brit hedged. So much for her fact-finding mission. Her heart wasn't in it tonight, anyway.

"Then make something up."

Brit laughed. "You would suggest that, Mr. Inventor."

"Come on, Brit. You can skip the details. Just tell me the important things, like where you're from and if you've been married and whether you rinse your toothbrush before you put the paste on. You know, the good stuff."

"Of course I rinse my toothbrush. The paste works into a better lather that way."

"I thought so. And the other questions?"

"I grew up on a farm in Iowa, and my best friend was Riley Dugan. Riley was determined to marry a rich man from the city, and she did. I righteously planned to marry a farm boy like my father, and I did. Riley and I argued about which was the better choice, yet neither of the marriages worked out."

"So the two chums banded together again."

"Yes."

"Never to part?" he teased.

Brit held out her finger for his inspection. "Never. See that little scar? That's where we became blood sisters."

"Where?" Harrison took her hand and bent his head to study her finger. "Oh, yeah, I think I found the spot." He traced a tiny circle on the sensitive skin.

"That tickles," Brit lied, trying to pull her hand from his. She wasn't ticklish, nor was his touch inspiring her laughter. Instead, a far different emotion coursed from her fingertips to the more elemental portions of her body.

He held her fast, letting his hand slip down to caress her wrist. "It does?" he asked innocently.

Speaking grew more difficult. "Well . . . not exactly," she managed.

"Mm," he murmured, watching her face as his finger drew a continuous figure eight on her skin.

She grew warm under his scrutiny. "Harrison?"

"I love that hollow spot at the base of your throat. I'd like to kiss you there."

"Harrison, we're—"

"In the middle of a restaurant. I know. And I can't even ask you home for a nightcap with a house full of kids and a snoopy Mrs. Weeples baby-sitting."

"Don't malign Mrs. Weeples. She saved my skin when Shane broke his arm."

"And beautiful skin it is, too." Harrison leaned forward. "Do you realize this is the first time all night we've mentioned the kids? I was afraid we'd spend the evening discussing them, but they haven't poked themselves into the conversation at all until now."

"That's true." She'd feared the same thing.

"I don't think you can classify this as much of a business dinner, if our business together is the house and kids."

"I guess not." Brit had trouble thinking straight as his caress continued lazily up the inside of her arm.

"I don't care."

"Neither do I." Brit met his gaze, allowing him to see the giddy emotion that was robbing her of rational thought. At this moment the threat of his domestic robot seemed insignificant compared to the banked fire of passion glowing in his eyes. In one evening she'd absorbed more about him and had learned to read his moods more accurately than in all the previous days she'd spent in his home. And right now his mood matched hers.

His touch on her arm reminded her all too well of their encounter earlier that evening, and she longed for a continuation of that wondrous experience. The excellent dinner and mellow wine had softened the edges of her caution. She wanted to be alone with Harrison Kent.

Brit took a deep breath. "Would you . . . like to go back to my place?"

A flame ignited in the depths of his dark eyes. "Yes." He relinquished her hand and reached for the check. "What about Riley?" he asked, throwing several bills onto the table and slipping his wallet into his back pocket.

"Riley?"

"You know. Your blood sister. Will she be out late?"

"Oh. Late. Yes, I think so. I think she said midnight."

"Good." He pushed back his chair and helped her from the table. Once more he held her jacket, but this time his lips found the nape of her neck as he settled the white fur around her shoulders. "You're delectable, Brit," he whispered.

"Mr. Kent?" The waiter appeared beside them.

Startled out of her romantic haze, Brit hastily stepped away from Harrison. She turned in time to see his frown of irritation.

"What is it?" he asked shortly.

"Telephone call."

Harrison and Brit looked at each other, both knowing Mrs. Weeples was the only person who knew where they were.

"You can take the call in the bar," the waiter announced.

"I'll wait here," Brit said.

Harrison caught her hand and squeezed it.

"Please do. Maybe she just wants to know how to work the VCR."

"Maybe." But Brit doubted it. As she watched Harrison follow the waiter to the bar, her heart wrenched at the knowledge that this tall, broad-shouldered man would not be hers to hold tonight. She felt selfish for the thought, especially because one of the children might be in real trouble. But oh, why did they have to be in trouble now?

Her hunch was confirmed by the look on Harrison's face when he returned.

"All hell's broken loose," he said with a grimace. "Mrs. Weeples tried to give Avery a bath, and Avery insisted on using the Scruffy-Scrubber."

"Oh, no. That's been malfunctioning all week."

"Avery must've thought I fixed it." Harrison took her arm as they hurried out of the restaurant. "Anyway, the Scruffy-Scrubber is spraying water all over the upstairs bathroom. Shane and Murphy got into a knock-down drag-out about how to fix it, and—"

"Not Shane's arm?"

"No, his nose. It's bleeding, which it does at the drop of a hat anyway, as you know, but Mrs. Weeples wanted to call the paramedics."

"Good Lord!"

"I told her to pinch his nose and hold it for ten minutes. With luck that crisis will be over by the time we get home, but the Scruffy-Scrubber has to be dealt with. I don't even have time to run you back home first. The place is flooding."

"I understand." Brit opened the car door for herself. Harrison was too preoccupied to remember the amenities of opening doors, of soft words and lin-

72

gering touches. The phone call from Mrs. Weeples had slammed a barricade against all the tender emotions and burgeoning passion Brit and Harrison had shared during the evening.

Brit felt like a child whose ice cream had fallen off the cone to the sidewalk. Damn that Avery, anyway, for demanding to use the Scruffy-Scrubber! Immediately Brit regretted thinking such angry thoughts about the little girl. Avery loved her father's myriad inventions and was proud to show them off. It wasn't her fault the Scruffy-Scrubber was broken. The timing was rotten, but who ever said life was fair?

"This is why I don't leave them very often," Harrison said, pushing the speed limit as he maneuvered through Washington traffic. "Something always goes wrong. Not everyone is equipped to handle those three."

"It's not just the kids. The inventions would throw most people for a loop even if the kids were perfect angels."

"That's ridiculous. They're time-saving machines, and anyone with a brain cell working would be glad to have them available."

Brit thought about mentioning that the Scruffy-Scrubber certainly hadn't saved much time tonight, but she decided that would be petty. Up until now, the evening had been lovely, and she tried to make her point diplomatically. "Not everyone reacts well to machines. Some people prefer the natural, human touch."

"Then they haven't adapted to the twentieth century."

Brit's goodwill began to evaporate. "I'd say your house operates in the twenty-first century."

"I'll take that as a compliment," he said tersely.

She opened her mouth to reply that it hadn't been intended as one, but she changed her mind and closed it again. The time had come for her to put aside her disappointment and irritation in the interest of survival. This was not the moment to reveal her antagonism toward his robotics project. He'd never confide in her if he knew her attitude, and he might just fire her. Then she'd have lost her chance to learn about the robot.

She'd also lose any chance of a relationship with Harrison Kent, but she wasn't prepared to admit how much that mattered to her. A half hour ago she'd been ready to fling herself into his arms, when a malfunctioning machine had intervened. How appropriate. Now she had time to collect herself and remember who Harrison was. Despite his dark good looks and the power of his beard-roughened kiss, this man was the enemy.

As they pulled into the Kent driveway, Murphy ran out to meet them.

"Dad, Dad! Water's dripping from the bathroom ceiling, and Avery's running around with no clothes on, and it wasn't my fault that Shane's nose started bleeding! Honest!"

"Calm down, Murphy," Brit said, putting an arm around the boy's shoulders as they hurried toward the front door. "Everything will be fine."

"Make Avery get dressed," Murphy pleaded. "She keeps running into the bathroom and playing in the spray. She wants Dad to fix the Scruffy-

Scrubber so it does this all the time. All Weeples-Creeples does is yell at her, but she doesn't pay attention."

"Murphy!" Harrison remonstrated. "Don't be disrespectful to Mrs. Weeples."

"Okay, Dad. But I don't want her to stay with us anymore. I want Brit."

"We'll see. Let's take care of this mess first."

"I'll handle Avery and Shane if you can turn off the Scruffy-Scrubber," Brit said firmly.

"Will do." Harrison jerked open the front door and took the stairs two at a time while he shrugged out of his dinner jacket. He almost ran into Avery skipping down the stairs, slippery as an otter from playing in the spray.

"Brit!" Avery cried, running to her with arms outstretched. "I've been having fun!"

"So I see." Brit took in the little girl's blue lips and wrinkled fingertips. Then she stooped down and gathered the wet little body against her furry jacket. "You wouldn't be getting cold, by any chance?"

"Not much. You smell nice, Brit. You look real pretty, too."

"Do you like this coat?"

"Yes." The tiny girl snuggled against her.

"Good. You can put it on." Brit was glad for the practical streak that had prompted her to buy a washable fake fur jacket.

"Oh, boy!" Avery wriggled away and held her arms straight as a scarecrow so Brit could put the jacket on her. The garment, hip length on Brit, came to Avery's ankles.

"You look just like a princess," Brit told her.

"I dunno," Murphy said. "I think she looks like" —he stopped speaking at Brit's warning look—"a princess," he finished.

"Right," Brit agreed. "Now let's go see how Shane's doing."

Avery caught her hand. "He's with Weeples-Creeples in the kitchen. You should see his shirt." The little girl rolled her blue eyes. "Yucky blood everywhere."

"Sh, Avery," Brit whispered. "Mrs. Weeples might hear you say that name."

Avery shrugged. "Doesn't matter. She won't be back. She's like all the others." Avery clung fiercely to Brit's hand. "Except you. You're the only one we like, Brit."

Shane's lanky body was draped over a kitchen chair. His head was tilted back, and Mrs. Weeples had a firm grip on his nose.

"Hi, Brit," Shane said in a nasal tone.

"Hi, Shane. Interesting decoration on your shirt."

"Yeah," Murphy interjected. "If he could wear it like that to school, he'd really gross some people out."

"Quiet, Murph."

"This boy scared me to death," Mrs. Weeples said in a voice grown hoarse with shouting.

Shane shifted uncomfortably. "Do you think that's enough with the nose, Brit?"

"How long's it been?"

Mrs. Weeples glanced at the wall clock. "Twenty-three minutes, ten seconds."

Brit hid a smile behind her hand. "I think that's long enough."

Mrs. Weeples relaxed her grip, and Shane sighed with relief.

"Just take it easy for a little while, Shane," Brit advised.

"I can't feel my nose," the boy complained, standing up. "I tried to get Mrs. Weeples-Cr—uh, Mrs. Weeples to use the Goody-Grabber to hold my nose, but she wouldn't."

"I should say not, young man!" Mrs. Weeples drew herself up indignantly. "I've never seen such a house. A machine for everything. I wouldn't be surprised at a machine to clip your toenails!"

"Dad's working on it," Murphy said seriously. "But it's still in the experimental stage. Right now it would chop your whole toe—"

"Spare me the details!" Mrs. Weeples threw both hands in the air. "I'm going home. When Mr. Kent needs a sitter, he'll have to call someone else."

Brit tried to soothe her. "We appreciate your coming over tonight, Mrs. Weeples. I doubt if it's always like this."

"No, it's probably worse! Lord knows I'm too old for this kind of nonsense. Cork-Torque. A metal dog with a bark mode. A vacuum cleaner named Bumpy." Shaking her head and mumbling, she headed for the front door. "Goody-Grabber, Scruffy-Scrubber. The place is booby-trapped!" The door slammed behind her.

"Hey, that's an idea," Murphy said. "If Dad gets anyone in here besides Brit, we'll set booby traps."

Harrison appeared in the kitchen, his sleeves rolled back and his shirt and slacks splotched with water. "Don't worry about that. I'm convinced that nobody supervises this household like Brit. She's quite handy to have around, wouldn't you guys agree?"

"Yes!" chorused the three children at once.

"In fact, she's so handy, I've decided she should stay here full time. We have that spare bedroom and bath downstairs. With Brit around twenty-four hours a day, I'd be able to devote more time to the robot project, and this entire household would run like a well-oiled machine. Weren't those your words when we met, Brit?"

Brit stared at him in shock. "I—yes, they were. But I don't—"

"Great. Then it's settled. I'll run you home, and you can spend the next day or so arranging things. From what I understand, your business is largely telephone work. You could do that as well here, couldn't you?"

"I really—"

Avery began to jump up and down, looking like a baby polar bear in the furry jacket. "Please, Brit. Please come live with us."

"Just until the robot's finished, of course," Harrison added.

"Of course," Brit said stiffly. *Live here?* The way Harrison proposed it, so nonchalantly in front of the kids, he obviously had no ulterior motives. He wanted a live-in Quintessential Woman to keep his household running like, as she had said, a well-oiled machine. That was it. She was a convenience to him, an extension of his corps of gadgets. No more hand-holding. No more romantic dinners. No more passionate kisses.

But wouldn't this arrangement provide exactly the opportunity she needed to learn the secrets of his newest invention? She would be solidly in the camp of the enemy—just where she wanted to be. All that romance garbage wouldn't help her save her business, anyway. Harrison's changed attitude was helping her see the correct path.

"I guess you'd better take me home so I can start packing," she said.

"Sure. We'll all go. Right, kids?"

"I get to ride in front with Brit," Avery chanted.

"Why not?" Brit said, heading for the door. Her silver lamé dress rustled and twinkled as she walked, but this time Harrison didn't seem to notice.

CHAPTER FIVE

"Ouch! Oh, Bumpy, it's you. Somebody must have left you out." Brit flipped on the kitchen light and rubbed her bruised shin. "Course, I should have turned the light on instead of stumbling around in the dark."

She paused in her verbal rambling to listen to another blast from the violent storm raging outside. The force of the thunder rattled the windows while lightning danced in a jagged, eerie light show all around the house. The commotion had awakened her, and as in her years on the farm, Brit had gotten up to make sure everything was all right.

Nudging the robot vacuum cleaner with her toe, she whispered, "Come on, Bumpy. You're going back where you belong. What Harrison needs to do is install a homing device on you. Then you can put yourself away if somebody forgets to. Oh, good grief. I must be bonkers! Less than a week of living in this crazy household, and I'm talking to the robots!" She laughed at herself and steered the mechanical thing toward the hall closet.

Frankly, Brit was pleased that in the week she'd been living with the Kents, none of the kids had been hurt; she'd managed to remain amiable with the various robots; and she'd kept up her own business adequately. Trouble was, she'd hardly seen Harrison. He'd been either working incessantly in his basement shop or off attending meetings or day-long seminars. Several times Brit had been caught in the position of decision maker simply because she was the adult in charge.

Another crack of thunder blasted from above, and the house was plunged into darkness. *There goes the electricity,* she thought. Lunging clumsily for the hall closet door, she shoved Bumpy inside.

At that point Brit heard another sound, a high-pitched wail. She lifted her head sharply as she recognized a child's cry.

Without stopping to analyze the situation, Brit raced up the stairs to Avery's room. The little girl lay in a rumpled hump in the center of the bed, quilt and bedspread pulled over her head, crying.

"Avery, Avery darling, what's wrong?" Brit gathered the weeping child into her arms and smoothed her tangled hair. "It's Brit, honey. Tell me why you're crying."

"I'm scared, Brit! Where's my daddy? There's too much noise everywhere!" Avery sobbed and clung to Brit. "And something's making noises outside my window!"

"I don't see a thing outside but trees, darling. Their branches are scratching your window, that's all. But don't worry, the window is closed tight," Brit murmured, rocking gently and keeping up a soft trail of soothing words. "There's nothing out there to be scared of, Avery darling. It's just a rainstorm kicking up a little thunder. I'm here with you, and we're safe and warm, just like woolly bears in a cave."

Avery sniffled. "What . . . what do woolly bears do when it rains?"

Brit pulled the child close and settled comfortably against the headboard. "Oh, they cuddle up together, just like we're doing, and pull the quilt up under their chins, and they sleep through the worst storms that blow through the woods."

"Do they get wet?"

"No, their cave keeps them dry, just like our house keeps us from getting wet. My little granny used to tell me this story. Once upon a time, high in the mountains, two little woolly bears named Boone and Gatlin got lost in a storm. . . ."

When the storm knocked out the electricity, Harrison obligingly closed up shop. He checked his watch, a marvelous gadget that held a data bank of information, including appointments, phone numbers, the date, and the time, and an optional hourly chime. It was after midnight. Damn, once again he'd lost track of time in his total devotion to the newest creation. He shut the door on his workshop and walked wearily past Brit's downstairs room. Curiously, the door was standing ajar, but she wasn't inside.

He proceeded through the house, thinking of the lovely woman he'd hired to take charge of his household. And of what an excellent job she'd done, too.

Brit. He had barely made time for her since she'd

been living there. But she had taken care of everything—and everybody—so competently, he'd been free to work full-time. In fact, it was amazing that in this brief time he'd come to rely so heavily on her. She was certainly someone special.

Harrison made his way through the dark house and paused at the foot of the front stairs. Did he hear voices above the storm? No, just one voice, a soft, female one. He took the stairs that led to the bedrooms and stood in the doorway to Avery's room. Brit's voice was like a gentle zephyr, soothing and sensuous. He leaned one shoulder against the doorframe and listened until she was finished.

". . . and Boone and Gatlin curled up in the cave and like all little woolly bears slept safe and warm throughout the long, cold winter."

All was silent for a moment, even the thunderstorm.

Satisfied that Avery was contentedly asleep, Brit eased slowly from the bed and covered the sleeping child. When she turned toward the doorway, a large, square-shouldered shadow loomed in the darkness, and she gasped.

Harrison took her hands and whispered, "It's just me. Don't panic."

"Harrison? Are the lights still out?"

"Yes. This storm's going strong," he said quietly, pulling her into the hallway. "Is Avery okay? Thunderstorms always bother her."

"She's asleep now," Brit whispered. "It woke me, too. I thought I'd check on things when I heard her crying."

"Do you always wander through the house when it storms?"

Brit smiled in the darkness. "Old habits are hard to break. On the farm, when it storms at night you generally need to make sure everything is tight."

"And you found everything tight around here except Avery?" He gazed over her shoulder into the little girl's room.

"In the middle of a stormy night sometimes a story works wonders."

"Apparently it worked for Avery. You're amazing, Brit. Thank you." He continued to hold her hands.

Brit shrugged self-consciously. "Well, I couldn't ignore a crying child."

"Especially when her father was too busy to hear her and give her the special attention she needed," Harrison muttered.

"I didn't mean that, Harrison. You have good reason to be so busy right now. The kids understand that."

"What would I do without you, Brit? What did I do before you arrived on my doorstep?"

"You left toys on the stairs and Bumpy in the middle of the kitchen for me to knock my shins against." She chuckled nervously, trying to lighten the moment.

Harrison didn't laugh. Instead he lifted her hands to his lips. "My sweet, efficient Brit. Are you all right? Need me to check your shins?"

"I'm fine, honest. I was just going to get a glass of milk and go back, uh, to bed."

"Since the lights are out, let me escort you back."

84

"Do you have any candles?"

"I have something better than candles," he said. "Matches in this household are dangerous. Come with me." He led her into another room. "Stand right here by the bed while I find it. I think Avery left it in the bathtub."

"In the bathtub? What is it? An iridescent sponge?" Brit chuckled, nervously aware that they were standing in Harrison's bedroom beside Harrison's bed. What kind of crazy gadget did he have that was better than matches?

"Iridescent sponge? No, but that's an idea."

Oh, Lord, now she was giving him even more ideas than he already had.

"You know how little girls are," he said cheerfully from the bathroom. "She and her little friends like to play make-believe behind the shower curtain." In a few moments, he appeared holding a round light that resembled a crystal ball.

On closer inspection, Brit could see that the sphere was decorated with odd shapes that were painted in contrasting colors. "What is it?"

Harrison grinned sheepishly. "The kids call it a Glo-Ball. Just touch it, and the world lights up. Patent's pending on it."

"Oh, I see. It's a real globe with all the countries outlined in different colors. How ingenious, Harrison." She gazed up at him in frank admiration. The low-beam light emitted by the Glo-Ball cast interesting shadows on his angular face. He hadn't shaved all day, and she could see where his dark beard shadowed his jawline. It made him look quite rugged and very masculine.

He shrugged. "It's a great gadget for kids because it's educational. But it also serves as a light when storms leave you in the dark."

She nodded, mesmerized by the mood of the night. She and Harrison were alone at last in his bedroom, during a violent spring storm. Everyone was asleep, and there was nothing—or no one—to keep them apart. "It's perfect for . . . certain occasions, Harrison."

He set the Glo-Ball on a nearby table and reached out to touch her hair. "Like now, Brit? You're very beautiful. Especially in this light." He moved closer.

She took in a shaky breath. "It's probably because you can't see that my hair's a mess and I don't have any makeup on."

He took off his glasses. Then both his large hands framed her face with his warm strength. "I like you natural, Brit." With agonizing slowness, he lowered his head to hers. Their lips met gently in a serene and patient kiss that was both unhurried and persuasive. "I like you just the way you are tonight."

Thunder crashed again as nature's fervor raged anew, and Brit knew her heart was pounding a beat that rivaled the storm outside. Instinctively she quivered, and he drew her closer. She could feel his warmth, sense his security. His appeal as a man was strong, and she found herself swaying toward him.

"You cold?" he asked. He slid his hands up and down her arms, then held her shoulders.

"Harrison, I don't think we should—"

"Sh," he whispered. "Don't think, Brit. Just let it happen."

A helpless moan slipped from her lips as he kissed

her again. This time, though, his lips were firm and convincing as they closed over hers. His tongue probed the inner sweetness of her mouth. As he kissed her, Brit responded, giving and receiving with joy she had never known before. She pressed fully against him, her breasts crushing against the hardness of his chest, her stomach meeting his taut belly, her thighs touching his.

He came to her hard and willing, a man desiring a woman. He hadn't denied it. And she couldn't help herself, couldn't resist him.

"I want you, Brit," he murmured between kisses. "I want you tonight."

Breathlessly she lifted her head and looked at him. "Do you think we should?"

"How can you ask that? You know I want you. And I feel you responding to me. You want me, too. We're both adults. We need each other tonight. Of course we should." His lips met hers again, hot and burning this time.

Fiercely they clung to each other, her lips opening for his tongue's intrusion. He dipped tentatively at first, then with fervor, into the dark, honeyed hollow.

She could feel him aggressive and aroused against her. Suddenly Brit wanted him with a desire that sizzled through her entire being, making her weak.

"Oh, Harrison," she murmured as his kisses trailed along her cheek and down her neck to the pulsing point at the base of her throat. She arched her back to make their closeness absolute and only then realized they were still fully clothed—he in a shirt and jeans, she in a robe and nightshirt. Oh,

87

that crazy nightshirt! She was hardly dressed appropriately for a tryst. But she had no time to think of it now.

He raised his head, and his eyes were darker than ever, dark with a raging passion. "Brit, I want you like I haven't wanted a woman in a long time."

Yes, Harrison, oh, yes . . . Oh, dear, she was weak in his arms.

"Harrison, maybe we'd better . . ." she began tentatively, but he kissed away her protests, and she forgot everything as their tongues danced together, teasing and playing at the sexy game. Their breath became heated and as one. Two hearts mingled and soared with passionate joy. Oh, yes, she wanted this man, wanted to know every inch of him, wanted him inside her.

His hands traveled down her body, exploring her back, searching for warm, intimate places. Even as she stood in his arms, she writhed with the erotic pleasure of his touch. Then he moved back, and a coolness filled the spot where he'd molded himself to her body.

"Undress for me, Brit," he muttered hoarsely, already stripping off his shirt.

Her eyes went to his body. Darkly tanned muscles gleamed in the soft twilight of the room. Like a woman possessed, she wanted to run her hands over every masculine inch of him.

She lifted her eyes uncertainly, a sudden vision of that raucous nightshirt haunting her. Why, oh why had she worn it tonight of all nights?

Harrison nodded, thinking he understood her hesitation. "I'll close the door." Harrison moved quickly to do the task, then stood before her. Waiting.

She stood there dumbly. That stupid nightshirt! But what could she do? He wanted to be her lover tonight. And she wanted him to be. She felt his gentle but firm hands pulling at her robe. Then it fell to her feet, revealing her less-than-romantic attire.

While Brit quivered in embarrassment, Harrison grinned good-naturedly. "What is this? My farm girl?"

Smiling wanly, Brit nodded and looked down. Her modest high-necked nightshirt was boldly emblazoned with the words FARMERS DO IT BETTER IN THE HAY. "I . . . I, oh, dear, I can't believe this is happening to me," she moaned.

"And you said you didn't blush," he admonished softly.

"Obviously I didn't plan on anyone seeing this nightshirt. It was a present from Riley, my roommate. I'm sure she never had this in mind, either."

"I don't have any hay handy tonight, but maybe my bed will do," he said teasingly. Gently he stroked her rosy, warm cheek, then fingered the narrow ruffled collar. "Come on, take it off for me, Brit."

Almost relieved to discard the embarrassing garment, she furiously loosened the three tiny buttons at the neck and slid the gown over her shoulders. It fell to the floor, leaving her shimmeringly nude.

Harrison's ebony eyes lit up, extolling her lush feminine beauty. Pert, uplifted breasts crested into full, ripe tips; a slender waist accentuated gently curving hips made for stroking; and there was a tantalizing downy delta at the juncture of her thighs. Ah, yes, she was more alluring than he had ever dreamed.

He reached out to touch her, letting his fingers trail sensuously over the swells of her breasts, then circle the inviting nipples. The tips were full and firm, tempting him to satisfy his hunger for her. "You're even more beautiful than I imagined, Brit. Oh, how I've thought of you like this."

She quivered beneath his erotic caresses and his blatantly sexy gaze. "When you touch me like that, Harrison, I feel hot all over."

"I want you to feel me all over your body. I want to touch you—no, to kiss you—everywhere." He unbuckled his belt, and the tiny rasp of his zipper pierced the sudden silence of the stormy night.

She licked her lips nervously and watched as he stepped out of his jeans. His body was muscular and boldly masculine in its arousal as he slid his briefs down. He moved one step closer to her, his eyes urging her into his arms. Slowly he pulled their passion-heated bodies together.

"I want you, Brit. There's nothing to stop us now."

"Nothing to stop us," she agreed, running her hands down the length of his back, gripping his firm buttocks.

A loud clap of thunder punctuated the brief lull in the storm, as if in tribute to what was happening between them.

He shifted away and ran his palm over the Glo-Ball. Immediately they were bathed in darkness. His arms slipped around her, sweeping her up against his chest. As he settled them into the center of the huge king-size bed, he murmured, "Brit, I can hardly wait for you."

She relaxed in his arms and let him come to her. He nibbled at her shoulders, then planted moist kisses around the aching mounds of her breasts. As his lips closed over the tips, taking each in turn, she made a soft kittenish sound and arched her breasts upward. He sucked the sweet morsels while one hand caressed her belly, her thighs, the soft delta between them. Then his lips followed the trail blazed by his hands, and his tongue did devilish things to her equilibrium.

"Oh, Harrison—"

"Easy, darling. Be still, and I'll make you feel wonderful."

But she couldn't do as he instructed, even though she tried. Unable to contain her burgeoning passion, she writhed joyously with his every advance. And he didn't stop until she had reached the brink of her endurance. When she moaned and gasped for air, he held back and let her passion recede, but just a little. Then he stroked her again in the most intimate and sensitive way until finally she begged for his fulfillment.

"Please, Harrison. Now! Now!"

Her knees parted, making a cradle for him, and he hovered over her, kissing and teasing her body with his. She arched upward to meet him, and he thrust forward, sliding gently into her softness. He held her very still until they had merged fully and completely. "Oh, yes, Brit. You are so nice and warm. We fit perfectly."

91

She wrapped her legs around his hips. "You feel so good with me. Like you belong."

"We belong together," he rasped, and began to move rhythmically inside her. He gathered speed and force, creating an inferno of desire and heat.

She joined his ecstatic journey, alternating her motions to match his until they rose in triumph. As one, they were transported to the ultimate euphoria, soaring, flying, dancing . . . until they floated back to the reality of each other's arms. They lay like that, entwined together, for a long time.

Finally he rolled to the side, his lips smiling faintly as he dozed. His arm cushioned her, and she snuggled closer, resting comfortably against his chest. When her eyelids fluttered shut, she felt at home right here with Harrison—living, sleeping, loving.

The storm continued to rage outside, but inside the Kent household everyone slept contentedly. It was a good sign. Everything was right with their world.

When early-morning fingers of sunlight spread over the foot of the bed, Brit awoke and wondered immediately about the prudence of her act. She caught her breath at the sight of Harrison, so darkly handsome against the sheets. She loved the shape of his mature, muscular body, sprinkled with dark hair; she loved what his body did to hers. With hers. He was a man with a fully developed passion, a deep passion meant just for her.

At least, last night his passion had been hers. But what about today?

She slid from the bed and began to rescue her

discarded clothes. What would their relationship be like now? How should she act? How would he? What did he think of her?

Gazing at the nightshirt with its romp-in-the-hay slogan, she groaned inside and pulled it on. She gave him one more wistful look. God, she was weak in his arms, totally unable to resist him. Maybe she should have resisted. But then she wouldn't have known the full joy of Harrison's passion. She'd never felt so thoroughly loved as in his bed last night.

What she wanted to do was to cuddle up beside him, to make love to him again, to show him the joy he'd shown her. To tell him how he made her feel.

But the kids would be getting up soon. She had to fix breakfast and send them off to school. It was part of her job. *Her job.* Had she jeopardized it by going to bed with her boss? It was certainly against her principles.

Brit hurried back to her room and a warm, quick shower. The night might have been Harrison's, but the day was her responsibility. Within half an hour, the kitchen was a bustling, chaotic mess.

"What's wrong?" She directed the question to Shane, who was studying his plate with distaste. "Go ahead. Tell me."

"I like my eggs cooked done, not runny like this."

"Oh, I forgot you don't like them sunny-side up. Sorry, Shane." She whisked his plate away and dumped the eggs back into the skillet.

"Hey, Brit, you burned the bacon," Murphy complained.

"Not burned, just extra crisp," Brit corrected. "It's good for you that way."

"Nobody likes limp bacon but you, Murphy. I like it supercrispy," Avery announced as she snapped off a bite. "Oh, hi, Daddy! Wanna bite of my bacon? Phew! What do I smell?"

"The cinnamon toast!" Brit shrieked and dashed for the oven. As she lifted the smoking pan to the stove top, the smoke detector went off, adding to the commotion. Brit groaned.

"I'll shut it off," Shane offered, and scrambled down the hall.

Harrison approached her and murmured gently, "Why don't you have a seat, Brit? I'll get us some coffee."

"I don't have time."

"Yes, you do. Now sit."

"But the toast—"

He poured two cups and directed her to the table. "Sit. And drink this. Just relax."

"I am relaxed!"

"No, you aren't. You stay put, and I'll take care of the toast. And everyone."

"Yes, but—"

"No arguing." Harrison admonished her with a wagging finger. "You've had a rough start today. Can't imagine why." He paused a moment to give her a sly gaze. "But we are grateful for the wonderful breakfasts you've prepared for us all week. When I'm in charge, breakfast is usually cold cereal." He finished dumping the charred toast and sat opposite Brit with his coffee.

Brit studied her cup. She knew what was bothering her, and it wasn't the kids or breakfast.

"I wanna go up to the mountains, Daddy. To see Boone and Gatlin," Avery chimed.

"Boone and Gatlin?" Murphy scoffed. "Who's that?"

"They're bears. Brit told me about them. They live in the mountains. And I wanna go see 'em."

Harrison grinned at Brit, recognizing what she'd done. "They sound like towns to me."

"Towns?" Murphy said. "Funny names for towns."

"Not really," Brit spoke up. "Boone is named after Daniel Boone, so it's a family name. Did you know there is even a town in the Smoky Mountains named Murphy? My little granny lived there before she married Grampa McIver and moved to Iowa."

"A town?" Murphy hopped up, scooting his chair back with a screech. "Oh, good grief! I hate my name even more now!" He grabbed his plate and plunked it down in the sink and dashed to his room.

They all sat in stunned silence for a moment, then Brit said, "I—I had no idea. I'd better go apologize." She started to rise, but Harrison put his hand on hers.

"No, let me. This is a long-standing family problem. I'll handle it." Harrison left the table with instructions for the other two kids. "Let's get a move on, gang. Finish up and brush your teeth."

Harrison calmed Murphy down, and in short order the Kent children bounded off to school. Finally, Brit and Harrison were alone.

Brit fumbled nervously with her coffee cup. "I

feel terrible about all this. I should never have said that to Murphy. I thought he would be delighted to think there was a town with his name. And as for the breakfast mess, I'm sorry."

He looked at her closely. "Burned toast isn't exactly a major disaster, you know, Brit."

"Oh, Harrison, I'm beginning to think we shouldn't have—"

He folded his arms against his chest. "You aren't having regrets, are you?"

"No! Well, I mean, maybe we'd better keep our distance. For the kids' sakes."

"What do they have to do with what's happening between us?"

"Well, I don't know. I—I just know we've made things very difficult."

"Not for me. Why do you have to analyze everything? Just let it happen naturally."

She cast her eyes downward. "I guess I'm scared, Harrison."

"Scared? Why?"

"Scared that I've ruined our working relationship. And everything else."

He slid his arms around her. "To hell with the working relationship. It's everything else that counts, Brit. Just us."

She tried to push away, but he held her securely. "No, Harrison. That's not exactly true. We have lots of other, uh, factors involved." She stopped short. Brit felt like a first-class heel. Not only did she feel scared, but she was overwhelmed with guilt. How could she tell Harrison she'd come here in the first place just to spy on him? Oh, she had overstepped the bounds of discretion. And she'd made the biggest mistake of all—falling in love with the enemy!

"What's wrong, Brit? What is going on inside that beautiful head of yours?"

She forced a smile. "Nothing. I'm just a little confused about us."

"Shall I straighten you out? We wanted each other. We slept together. What we shared was very special to me."

"It was very special to me, too, Harrison," she admitted truthfully. "But I need some time to sort this out."

The phone rang, and Brit pushed away from him. "Anyway, the Quintessential Woman's day starts now." She reached for the phone. When she returned, Harrison was finishing his coffee and a fresh piece of toast.

"How long do you need to think about us?"

"At least this weekend."

"Okay, fair enough. Maybe we both need this time apart. Just be sure to come back Sunday night, Brit. We need you." He paused and his serious ebony gaze caught hers. "I need you."

She swallowed hard and nodded. It had crossed her mind not to return to the Kent household. But in her heart Brit knew she couldn't leave him. Not yet.

CHAPTER SIX

Brit half expected Harrison to be more attentive during the day, considering that tomorrow and Sunday she'd be back at her apartment thinking about whether to continue their relationship. But he didn't make any effort to be with her. Apparently Harrison could tune Brit out of his life whenever he chose. The idea bothered her.

By four in the afternoon, with all three kids home from school, Brit was too busy to give any more thought to Harrison's behavior.

"There's lunch meat and bread here," she instructed Shane. "If your father forgets about meals this weekend, you can make sandwiches."

"Why can't you stay?" Murphy complained. "It'll be a real zoo around here without you."

"So what else is new?" Shane countered, biting into a cookie.

Brit ruffled Murphy's brown hair. "You three can handle it. I need a couple of days each week to do a few things around my apartment. Besides, you'll appreciate me more when I come back."

"I 'preciate you," piped Avery as she clomped

around the kitchen in Brit's purple polka-dot shoes. "I wish you were my mommy."

Shane glared at the little girl. "Zip your lip, Avery."

"Why should I?" She faced her brother, hands on hips. "You and Murph said the same thing yesterday."

Shane reddened and glanced at Brit. "Yeah, but we didn't go blabbing it in front of Brit."

Brit smiled, touched by their affection for her. "That's okay, Shane. I'm honored that you think so highly of me. But I'm not your mother; I'm a hired employee. Your dad and I agreed to my taking weekends off, both to save him money and to give me some free time."

Avery's brow wrinkled in confusion. "Daddy pays you money to take care of us?"

"Yes."

"I thought you did it for free."

"I'd like to, sweetheart, but I couldn't afford to give my services away." Brit spread her hands. "Then I'd be broke."

"Oh." Avery lifted her wide blue gaze. "But if you weren't broke, you'd do it for free, wouldn't you?"

"I suppose I would," Brit admitted.

"Because you love us, right?"

Brit's eyes misted. "Yes."

"I knew it," Avery crowed happily, throwing her tiny arms around Brit's waist.

Brit hugged the little girl and smoothed her bright hair. Of course she cared for these children. They were terrific kids. Despite the inevitable problems they caused, they were bright and affectionate, fun to be around, easy to love. Just like their father. The comparison jolted her as if she'd touched a live electric wire. Was she falling in love with Harrison Kent?

Avery peered up at Brit. "And you're gonna have a birthday party for Murph, aren't you?"

Brit fought to understand Avery's question as the possibility that she loved Harrison played havoc with her concentration. She couldn't love him! He was the enemy. And yet—Brit's heart lurched—she did. Oh, God.

"Aren't you having a party?" Avery prompted.

"Yes, yes of course." Brit took a deep breath and glanced at the younger boy. "When is your birthday, Murphy?"

"Week after next." Murphy scuffed the floor with the toe of his tennis shoe. "But that's okay. You don't have to do anything special."

"Why, of course I do! Birthdays are very important." Brit tried to push thoughts of Harrison away. "Let's see, I bet you'll be ten years old."

"Yep." His eyes shone proudly. "Double digits."

"That's quite an accomplishment, Murphy. I don't know how you celebrate birthdays in this house, but when I was a kid we had balloons, and a fancy cake, of course, and the birthday person could choose the dinner menu, and—"

Shane interrupted her. "We used to do stuff like that, but Dad doesn't always remember birthdays."

Brit's mouth dropped open. She was falling in love with a man who forgot birthdays? "You're kidding."

"He's pretty busy," Shane defended. "And he tries to remember—but you know Dad, the absent-minded professor."

"Yeah," Murphy agreed. "Last October he didn't remember Shane's birthday until two days later. He bought a big cake and two kinds of ice cream, but it still didn't feel much like a party."

Brit frowned. "I should say not. Two days late, indeed! Things will be different this time, Murphy. You can count on it." No matter whether she loved Harrison or not, she wanted to throttle him. Forgetting a child's birthday was high on her list of unforgivable sins.

Avery hopped up and down, jumping right out of her high heels. "Oh, boy! A party, a party!"

"While I'm gone this weekend, think about what kind of party you want, Murphy," Brit said. "And presents. Think of what presents you'd like." If she had anything to say about it, Murphy would have the best celebration of his life. Harrison should be strung up by his thumbs for treating birthdays so casually!

Shane laughed. "Get him some stilts. Murph the Smurf needs stilts so he won't be such a shrimp."

"Don't call me Murph the Smurf!"

"Why not? It fits."

"Someday I'm gonna grow, Shane Kent, and when I do I'm gonna punch you in the nose harder than the last time, and I hope you never stop bleeding!"

"Boys, that's enough."

"I hate it when he calls me that, Brit. And I hate

my stupid name. No regular guys are ever named Murphy. Yuck!"

"Your name is distinctive, Murphy."

He looked at her with suspicion. "What do you mean *distinctive?* It sounds like *stink* to me."

Shane snickered.

"It means your name is different, unique," Brit told Murphy while she chastised Shane with a disapproving glance.

"What'd I tell you?" Murphy cried. "I don't want to be different!" He whirled and stomped out of the room.

"I want you to stop calling him Murph the Smurf," Brit said sternly to Shane.

"Aw, it's such a great name."

"Would you like to be called that?"

Avery giggled. "I would. Smurfs are so cute. 'Cept I'd be a Smurfette."

"At this point in his life, Murphy doesn't want to be cute," Brit said. "So cut it out, Shane."

"I'll try. But it sounds terrific together, doesn't it? Murph the Smurf, Murph the Smurf."

"Murph the Smurf, Murph the Smurf," chanted Avery.

"Enough!" Brit sent them both scorching looks. "By Monday I want that nickname out of both your vocabularies."

"Okay," Shane agreed reluctantly. "But it won't be easy. Hey, are you going to tell Dad about this party?"

"Certainly."

"If you don't want him to forget, I'd tape a note to his bathroom mirror," Shane advised.

"That's a good idea, Shane. Don't worry, I won't let him forget." She'd tape a note to his gorgeous nose if necessary. And very soon she planned to tell him what she thought of a man who forgot his own children's birthdays.

But not this afternoon. Not after she'd admitted to herself that she was in love with him. Monday, after a weekend apart, they could both be more rational about lots of things, including the passion that had consumed them last night.

All weekend long, Brit dutifully fought to apply careful logic to her situation with Harrison. She failed miserably. Reason had no chance when her mind was filled with images of Harrison lying next to her, stroking her, whispering soft words of endearment. When she closed her eyes he was there, stripping her clothes off, reaching for her. . . .

Instead of arriving at the Kent house Sunday night with her emotions cooly in check, Brit was a jangled mass of nerves. She feared that as soon as the object of her weekend fantasies walked into the room, she might fall into his arms and beg him to make love to her.

But Harrison didn't give her the chance. Instead, he stayed secluded in his workshop Sunday evening —as if her return were of scant importance to him. She had stewed over how to handle his anticipated knock at her bedroom door during the night, but it never came. She slept fitfully.

In the morning she dressed in her normal work clothes, a pair of khaki slacks, and a matching short-sleeved sweater. Although she hadn't seen

Harrison last night, he usually came down for breakfast on weekday mornings. After the kids left for school, Harrison would probably expect an answer about their relationship, and she wanted to look as businesslike as possible for the ensuing discussion.

However, her boss gulped his breakfast and hurried back to his lair with little more than a glance in her direction. Brit realized he was deliberately avoiding her. He wanted her to initiate the next encounter, and if she chose, they could remain relative strangers until the robot was finished and her job was over. A smart woman would leave it at that.

But what about Murphy's birthday party? She could organize it all by herself, but that wouldn't mean as much to the boy as having his father in on the celebration, too. Besides, Harrison needed to learn that he couldn't ignore important events in his children's lives. Brit felt an obligation to right that wrong before she left, no matter what else happened. She owed it to the kids.

Armed with righteous indignation, hoping it camouflaged her more volatile feelings toward Harrison, Brit headed for the basement workshop and rapped briskly on the door.

"Come in, Brit."

She opened the door. "How did you know who it was?"

"It had to be you. You wouldn't send someone else down here without checking with me first. You're too efficient for that."

She stared at him in silence. He had swiveled away from the workbench and was facing her, knees apart, feet hooked on the rungs of the stool. The dark chest hair that had played such a part in her fantasies for the past three nights curled from the open neck of his yellow knit shirt.

"Harrison, we need to talk."

"Yes, we do." He stood up, a flicker of desire in his ebony eyes.

Brit took a step backward in sudden panic. The workshop was dark and intimate, with the only light shining on Harrison's workbench. She knew he had a bed down here for the nights he worked straight through, taking only cat naps in between inspirations. If he touched her now, they wouldn't talk. And she wanted to discuss Murphy.

"It's almost lunchtime," she said, reaching behind her for the doorknob. "Why don't we talk over a sandwich or a bowl of soup?"

"That's fine." The light of interest in his eyes died, and his expression became impassive. "As a matter of fact, we have a new kitchen gadget I worked on this weekend. The kids call it Sandy Sandwich. We can try it out. And the little robot needs a run, so we can have him serve us the meal. I'll get my remote control switch box."

"No." The word was out before she knew it.

He turned. "Why not?"

"Let's—let's pack a picnic lunch and walk down to Wolf Trap. And I'll make the sandwiches. Maybe we both need to get away from all these machines."

He studied her for a moment. "Okay, but we should probably take the Fly-Zapper and the Ant-Sucker. And I have a motorized picnic basket that—"

"No machines, Harrison!"

He threw up both hands. "Okay, okay. No machines. A little touchy on the subject, aren't you?"

"Sometimes I prefer human power, that's all."

"Inefficient."

"Natural. A few bugs are required on a real picnic. But let's not fight about it, Harrison. If you'll find a blanket and an ordinary basket, I'll fix the lunch." As long as she was organizing an activity, she felt more in control. It was a lovely day for an outing, and besides, outdoors was safer territory for their discussion than inside a quiet house with no children and lots of privacy.

Brit had the meal prepared by the time Harrison found a blanket and basket. His machines were always underfoot, she mused, but everyday items required a concentrated search. Mrs. Weeples was right—the Kent household was strange.

"How about some wine?" Harrison suggested, taking a bottle of Chablis from the refrigerator.

"Do you have an ordinary corkscrew?"

"Somewhere." He rummaged through a drawer. "If not, I'll use my teeth. Anything but the Cork-Torque, right?"

Brit laughed. "Right."

He continued to sort through the kitchen utensils in the drawer. "I like to hear you laugh," he said softly.

She didn't respond. Better to ignore such personal allusions, she decided, until they were well away from the house, well away from Harrison's king-size bed that tempted her so insidiously.

"Aha!" he crowed, holding aloft a metal cork-screw. "Is this primitive enough for you?"

"Perfect." Brit took the item and tossed it into the basket without meeting his gaze. "I think that should do it. Let's go."

They took the path that led from behind the house across a wooded ravine to Wolf Trap, a grassy amphitheater with an elaborate open-air stage where many well-known performers entertained each summer. The kids had shown Brit the path during the three days she spent alone with them, but she allowed Harrison to lead the way. He carried the picnic basket easily under one arm, and Brit admired the ripple of his shoulder muscles as he adjusted the basket against one hip.

"The trees are budding," she remarked, breathing deeply of the moist, fragrant air. "The woods smell wonderful this time of year."

"A little like that perfume you wore the night we had dinner," Harrison added.

"I suppose." Brit's fingers dug into the blanket she was carrying. Maybe she'd better broach the subject of Murphy immediately and try to sidetrack Harrison's subtle reminders of their attraction to each other. "The main reason I wanted to talk to you today was to discuss Murphy's birthday."

"Murphy's birthday?" He put out his hand to help her across a gurgling stream. When she took it, he pulled her close to his side and smiled. "You're not serious, Brit. I can't believe you dragged me out into this spring day to discuss the kids."

"Uh, yes. Mostly." She backed away and disen-

107

gaged her hand. His touch was like a match to kerosene. "Murphy's birthday is next week, and—"

"That soon? He can't be a year older already."

Her original indignation flared. "Just as I thought, Harrison Kent. You would have missed another birthday. Shame on you."

"Pam always took care of those things. I'm not very good at it."

"That's a cop-out, and you know it. Birthdays are very important to children, Harrison. And they must be celebrated on the exact day, not a few days later."

He grinned sheepishly. "They told you, huh?"

"Yes, and I was horrified. That can't happen again."

"And you're here to see that it doesn't." He turned up the path again. "Okay, what are your plans?" he asked good-naturedly.

"Oh, no you don't. I won't let you turn it over to me. You have to help make plans, and Murphy should know that you're involved."

Harrison turned his head and winked at her. "Doesn't the Quintessential Woman do birthday parties?"

"Yes, of course. But this is different, Harrison. Murphy needs to know that you care enough to plan part of the celebration."

"Mm."

They emerged from the trees and spread the blanket on a grassy spot overlooking the bandshell. While Harrison struggled with the corkscrew, Brit unpacked croissants stuffed with crabmeat salad, a container of sliced cheese and fruit, and two wine-glasses.

With a muffled curse, Harrison pulled half of the cork out of the bottle; the rest fell in bits and pieces into the Chablis. "The Cork-Torque would never have made such a mess," he mumbled, pouring the glasses full.

Brit tried to pick a tiny piece of cork from the surface of her wine. "The Cork-Torque requires electricity."

"No, it doesn't. It runs on batteries, too. I've designed my inventions so they can operate anywhere."

"I'm impressed." She captured a floating bit of cork on her finger and shook it off onto the grass. Then she licked the wine from her finger.

"I bet you're impressed."

She glanced up and caught the quickly hidden spark of desire in his dark eyes. "No, I really am. Except that once in a while it's nice to listen to natural sounds instead of a motor whirring. Do you hear that bird giving us a concert?"

"Yeah. Avery's been after me to make her one. If I had my recorder, I'd tape that song, so I could—"

"Harrison."

"Yes, Brit?"

"Can you forget inventions for once? You seem to have them permeating your life."

"Not true."

"It most certainly is," Brit maintained stoutly. "You've got machines in every—"

"There aren't any in my bedroom."

She stared at him for a long moment, unable to

speak as images of that bedroom and the passion they had shared there flashed before her. Yes, God help her, she loved him.

"You see," he continued softly, holding her gaze with his own, "I like some things perfectly natural, too."

She swallowed heavily. "I . . . I think we were discussing Murphy's birthday."

"Were we?"

"Yes." Her voice steadied. "And having you help. It's very important, Harrison."

He smiled and looked at her quietly for a breathless space of time. Then he sat up straighter and squared his broad shoulders. "You're right, of course. I should help. Can I be in charge of games?"

Brit felt relieved and disappointed at the same time. He was following her lead. Wasn't that what she wanted? "In charge of games," she repeated, rolling her eyes. "Dare I turn you loose on games with your imagination? No telling what you'll have us all doing."

"You said you wanted me to be in on this."

"So I did. Okay. We're at your mercy."

"I like the sound of that." Behind the narrow rim of his glasses his gaze grew warm and inviting once more.

Brit twisted her napkin nervously. "You wouldn't take advantage of the situation, would you?"

"I wouldn't dream of it." He raised his glass. "To Murphy's birthday."

"To Murphy's birthday." Brit clinked her glass with his and sipped her wine. How lovely it was here, drinking wine on a grassy hillside with Harri-

110

son Kent. If only there were no house full of kids, no robot, no complications.

"The croissants are great," Harrison praised, taking another bite.

"Yes, they are," she acknowledged with a smile. She ate hers hungrily, wondering if unsatisfied desire had increased her appetite.

"And they taste so much better because I know you made them with your own hands."

"You're teasing me."

"Not really. You have a point." He finished his croissant and reached for a slice of apple. "The picnic without machines was a good idea, Brit. I become so involved with my robotic projects that I forget how beautiful a spring day can be."

An unwanted picture of Harrison as a young husband flashed into Brit's mind. Had he and Pam shared picnics, bottles of wine, laughter? Of course they had.

"What was she like?" Brit asked without thinking.

"Who?"

"Never mind. I have no right to—"

"Of course you do." His eyes were gentle. "You want to know about Pam, don't you?"

She nodded.

"You would have liked her. She was always smiling, and she loved to cook—a fact she blamed for the extra five pounds she couldn't seem to lose."

Brit listened, wanting and yet not wanting to hear about the woman Harrison had once loved, probably still loved. Brit decided that not only was her behavior with Harrison unprofessional, it was foolish. She could never hope to compete with a cherished memory.

"You know," Harrison continued, "sitting here reminds me of all the Wolf Trap performances Pam and I enjoyed. I haven't been back in a long time. We'll have to do that."

"I don't think so." The food that moments ago had tasted so good lost all its appeal for Brit.

"Why? Are you allergic to mosquitoes or something?"

"No. But under the circumstances, I don't think we should date or . . . anything."

"Oh?" He set his wineglass on top of the picnic basket and faced her. "What circumstances?"

"For one thing, it hasn't been that long since you lost your wife."

He reached for her hand. "Listen, Brit. I loved Pam. Her death was the worst thing that has ever happened to me, and for a long time I didn't want anything to do with another woman. But that time is past. I have the natural urges of any healthy man, and believe me, you stimulate those urges like crazy."

"And I can't deny that I'm . . . attracted to you, but—"

"Then what's the problem?" He lifted his hand to stroke her cheek. "We need each other, Brit. I can't forget how you felt beneath me Thursday night. It's been hell trying to concentrate on the robot."

"I didn't notice you having any trouble."

He laughed shortly. "Did you think because I spent most of my time in the workshop that I was working? I'm embarrassed to admit how many hours of that time were spent daydreaming about you and how soft your skin feels."

Brit dropped her gaze, but he tilted her chin up so she had to look at him.

"I want you, Brit. Right now, in fact. But I suspect you planned this public meal so we wouldn't get carried away. Why won't you just let it happen, Brit? Didn't you enjoy Thursday night?"

"Yes." Her voice was hoarse. "But going to bed with my boss was very unprofessional."

He smiled. "No one will ever hear of it from me. I keep secrets like you wouldn't believe. They could shove splinters under my fingernails, chop off my little toe, anything, and I wouldn't tell."

She shook her head, smiling back at him in spite of herself. "The fact that you and I know is problem enough."

"We sort of have to know, Brit, if we're the ones involved."

"That's it—we shouldn't be involved. Not sexually. It goes against my principles."

"I don't understand why. I know you don't make a practice of sleeping with your clients, and I'm damned glad you don't. But is your value system so rigid that you can't allow an exception this time? We have something pretty special here, Brit."

"I know." She felt heartsick because she couldn't tell him the whole truth, that she had taken on this job in order to spy on him. The way she saw it, her success with the Quintessential Woman depended on his failure with his domestic robot. When he found out about her, it would be painful enough without the added complication of a love affair.

113

Brit also knew that the confrontation over the robot wasn't far away. In the short time she'd been in Harrison's workshop this morning, Brit had taken note of the large machine lying on his workbench. Sure, wires hung out and pieces still lay around waiting to be attached to the mechanical creature. But her nemesis had a definite form now with an intimidating bank of controls. Was it capable of replacing her? Soon she'd know.

"What is it, Brit? What is so terribly wrong with enjoying what we have together?"

He wouldn't understand unless she told him everything, and she couldn't do that. "It's—unprofessional, that's all. For both our sakes, let's keep this attraction between us in check."

"Too late for that, I'm afraid. You already came to my bed and taught me how wonderful our lovemaking can be. I'd be a fool not to want you back there again." He stroked the inside of her elbow. "And I'm no fool. Come home with me, Brit. The kids won't be back for two hours."

She summoned all her willpower and turned away from the velvet seduction of his touch. "Then I guess it's all up to me. I'll have to enforce my own personal rules of conduct if you won't help."

"If you think you can."

She tossed her hair back from her shoulders. "Of course I can."

"I wouldn't be so sure. After Thursday night, I know the Quintessential Woman is more than efficient. She's also passionate and lusty."

"When she chooses."

His low chuckle rumbled between them, sending shivers of desire up her spine.

Ignoring her body language that announced she didn't want to be touched, he caught her chin and turned her face toward him, forcing her to meet the dark challenge of his gaze.

"You really think so?"

"Yes," she whispered.

Lightly he brushed her trembling lips with his own before lifting his head to watch the fire ignite in her eyes.

His voice was a caress. "Don't kid yourself, Brit."

CHAPTER SEVEN

Brit found that living with Harrison—and trying to avoid him—were not easy tasks. Instead of living in his workshop as he had in the past, the man seemed to be everywhere now, all the time, especially at meals. Breakfast with the kids *and Brit* became a social occasion. He proposed daily walks and lunch *with Brit,* just for fun. And dinner was a time for catching up with the kids' day, then lingering over coffee *with Brit.*

Admittedly, she enjoyed every minute with Harrison. In fact, that worried her. How could she accomplish her original mission of keeping an eye on her nemesis, the ultimate robot, with Harrison always there? What would happen when "the thing" was completed and she had to leave the Kent home? The way she felt now about Harrison, how could she simply walk away? And yet she knew she must.

By midweek, Brit had more immediate worries, such as how she would make it until Friday without falling into Harrison's welcome and eager arms. He was particularly chipper Wednesday morning and drew her aside after the kids had trooped merrily away to school.

"What about lunch in Wolf Trap Park today?"

"I'm too busy, Harrison."

"I'll pack the sandwiches."

"Thanks, but I really don't have time."

"I'm the boss," he countered. "I'll give you time."

"I didn't plan to be here all day. I have a million errands to run."

"I'll drive you. Together we'll get them done in half the time. Then we'll be free for—"

"Please, Harrison. You're making this very difficult."

He turned away from her, grabbed a chair, and straddled it angrily. "Damn it, Brit! Don't you see how much I want to be with you?"

She began clearing the breakfast table and tried to keep her voice light. "You're with me morning, noon, and night."

"Alone," he grated.

Brit piled dishes in the sink. "Harrison, I told you, I don't think it's a good thing for us to—"

Suddenly his strong arms were circling her from behind, his hands caressing her forearms. "I thought it was very good when we were alone, Brit."

His deep voice reverberated through her, and she trembled at the renewed sensations. She knew he was talking about more than just sipping coffee together with no interruptions. In a tremulous voice, she admitted, "Yes, it was wonderful. But that was a weak moment for both of us."

"Thank God for weak moments," he said, chuckling softly as he rubbed her arms and kissed a particularly tender spot on her neck. "I'm glad we both feel the same way about what happened between us."

His hands slid to circle her waist; his arms were like tempered steel around her ribs. She tried to resist, but her heart pounded with increased excitement as he drew her closer. She cleared her throat in an attempt to sound decisive. "But, Harrison, don't you also see that it's dangerous?"

He gripped her shoulders and turned her around to face him. "Dangerous? This is dangerous?" He lowered his head to kiss her lips lightly. "I see it as beautiful, Brit. As beautiful as you."

His lips claimed hers, fully dominating them, persuading them apart for his exploring tongue. The touch was gentle and demanding at the same time.

Brit weakened, allowing herself a moment of sublime pleasure in Harrison's arms. Her lips melded softly with his as the sweet flame of desire flickered and swelled between them. Her body swayed against his, daring to seek his masculine strength. His large, strong hands explored the length of her back, continually pressing and molding her to him, holding her securely.

She felt his heart beating soundly against her breast, and she arched to increase that pleasant throbbing. Somehow her arms defied all her verbal denials and crept up to his shoulders. Her fingers spread into the soft hair at the base of his neck, and she relished the feel of his rugged, masculine body.

Lost to time and place, aware of nothing but the wildfire sensations raging between them, Brit and Harrison stood locked together in the kitchen. They remained like that for a long, glorious moment, passionately entwined, until music rang repeatedly in their ears.

The theme from *Rocky* played again, and Brit suddenly realized that what she had heard was the doorbell. "Uh-oh," she mumbled, forcing herself away from the kiss, "the cleaning crew. They're here to clean the carpet."

"To hell with the carpet," Harrison rasped, trying to pull her back into his embrace.

"Oh, no, Harrison. It must be done. And I have to supervise."

"There's only one thing I want you to supervise, Brit. You and me."

"I can't, Harrison. I have to go now." She broke contact with him and backed away a step and fluffed her hair with one hand. "I . . . must. They're here, and—"

"Brit, I need to talk to you. I want you Friday night—"

She waved a hand to him as the first eight notes of the *Rocky* theme resounded through the house again. "Can it wait?" She halted. "What did you say? You want to make an appointment for us— Harrison!"

"No, it's not what you think. I've been invited to a state dinner on the Hill, and I'd like you to go with me. It's very important to my career."

She hesitated, and that was her downfall. He looked so handsome with his hair slightly disheveled and that lustful gleam still alive in his ebony eyes. "I—I have a party to cater Friday night. But I guess we can work something out."

119

He smiled with relief. "Great. I really want to take you. Now you'd better let the carpet cleaners in before the *Rocky* tape self-destructs."

"Right." She nodded and wheeled around, straightening her blouse and trying to assume an in-charge expression. But her lips still tingled from Harrison's kiss. And her heart pounded excitedly at the thought of going out with him again. Alone.

"Why is this always so difficult for us? All I want to do is attend a dull but important dinner party on the Hill. With you, Brit. Incidentally, you look lovely."

"Thank you," she murmured. "It's blue."

"Does it match your eyes?"

"Yes." She nodded shyly in the darkness of the car.

His voice lowered. "I may not be able to distinguish colors, but I have an active imagination."

She grinned at that truth and changed the subject to something less personal. "Did you have trouble getting a sitter for tonight, Harrison?"

"Hell, it takes a management specialist to arrange a little private time with you, Brit. My kids seem to occupy—and complicate—almost every facet of my life."

Brit smiled across the car seat at him as they rolled down Arlington Boulevard. "That's typical. Didn't anyone ever tell you three children are a handful?"

"My mother constantly reminds me," he retorted. "Tonight before I picked you up, I had to drop Avery at a friend's to spend the night. Then I

120

took Shane and two friends and three hundred pounds of camping equipment to meet the Scouts for an overnight camping trip. They're only staying one night, yet they had enough stuff for a month-long encampment at Valley Forge. Mrs. Weeples is home with Murphy."

"You're a good dad," Brit patronized with a teasing smile. "How did you persuade Mrs. Weeples to baby-sit again? I thought she was a goner last time."

"I think bribe is the correct word for it. I'm paying her double!"

"That's nice of you, Harrison."

"Now that we're on our way, could we forget about the kids for a few hours? I'd like to have an adult conversation for a change."

The car phone rang as if to defy his statement.

"Why didn't I disconnect this thing?" Harrison grumbled as he punched the button that allowed the call to come through a conference speaker without bothering with a receiver. "Yes? Kent here."

"Dad? Murph here." The boy's voice resounded loudly.

"Yes, Murph, what is it, son?"

Murphy's frantic voice came pleading over the airwaves. "Dad! This is an emergency! Tom got out! And Mrs. Weeples is—uh, she's yelling from up on top of the dining-room table. She claims she won't come down all night if I don't find him. But I can't find him and—"

"That mouse again?" Harrison expelled angrily, then gained more control. "Okay, son, take it easy! We'll be right there. And tell Mrs. Weeples to calm down. We're on our way back."

"Thanks, Dad."

Harrison did a quick U-turn as soon as he could and gunned the accelerator, mumbling to himself.

Brit placed her hand on his arm as he steered recklessly through traffic. "Harrison, slow down. It won't help Murphy if you have a wreck on the way. It won't help us, either."

He took a deep breath and slowed the car. "You're right, Brit. Sorry. It's just that tonight has been so hectic, and now a damned mouse—"

"I know, I know," she soothed. "But we'll manage. And we'll make it to the dinner. We'll just be a little late."

"Of all nights, why tonight? Why now?" He gripped the steering wheel angrily and fumed.

"I figured he'd escape sometime," Brit offered softly. "It was inevitable."

Harrison gestured with growing irritation. "This is not the first time it's happened. But it's the last! Tom is the only live pet I have allowed in the house because Murphy swore he'd keep him in his room and take complete care of him—and see that he didn't escape."

"I'm sure it was an accident, Harrison."

"It always is. Each time, Murph swears it won't happen again. Tom is the remaining half of a matched pair. Jerry became a free agent a few months ago when he escaped out the front door. It was crazy at our house with Murph running down the street, calling Jerry, and Avery running behind him bawling!"

"I can imagine."

122

He shook his head in frustration. "And now Tom's scaring the devil out of Mrs. Weeples!"

"Poor lady!" Brit giggled, unable to keep a straight face. "If it's not robots running amok, it's kids or a mouse!"

"Wonder how much this'll cost me. She'll probably charge triple for the emotional stress," Harrison grumbled. "And we have to find him all decked out in our party clothes!"

Murphy met them at the door, a worried frown on his young face. "Sorry to spoil your evening, Dad. But Mrs. Weeples made me call you. She said she doesn't want to spend the whole night sitting on the table."

"Can't say that I blame her, son." Harrison walked into the dining room to comfort Mrs. Weeples, who was making noises they could hear all the way into the living room.

Murphy looked so woebegone that Brit felt obliged to try to cheer him up. "Did you know that finding mice is my specialty, Murph?"

"Oh, yeah? How come?"

"My youngest brother always had some furry little thing in his room, and whenever it got loose, he'd get me to help him find it before Grandma found out. Grandma was a little bit like Mrs. Weeples," she confided with a grin. "Now, where did Tom disappear?"

"I think he's up here." Murphy led the way upstairs to his father's bedroom.

Brit smiled at the thought of the tiny creature seeking refuge in Harrison's room. "First thing you do is close the door. In case we flush him out, he can't escape this room."

Half an hour later, the three of them were still down on all fours, making funny noises and encouraging the tiny mouse to become a captive again. However, Tom stubbornly refused to go willingly. Brit, her royal blue taffeta dress hiked up to her thighs, rammed a broom handle under the bed. Harrison, who had carefully removed his white dinner jacket, knelt on sharply creased trousers. His job was to make sure Tom didn't escape on the opposite side.

Murphy crumbled cheese down the maze they had constructed of old shoes, baseball bats and gloves, books, and anything else that could possibly block a small mouse. "He's coming this way!" Murphy whispered excitedly. "Come on, Tom."

Brit held her breath as the furry brown creature with the stringy pink tail nibbled its way to the shoebox at the end of the maze.

"Yippee!" Murphy yelled as he clamped the lid down. "Thanks, Dad. Thanks, Brit."

Harrison glared sternly at his young son. "Murphy John Kent, if this happens again, I'll have to—"

"Oh, Dad, it won't. Never again! I promise!"

"I've heard that promise before, Murph." Harrison gathered the broom and his dinner jacket and headed downstairs. "I'm going to see if I can calm Mrs. Weeples and help her down from the dining-room table. We'll talk about Tom tomorrow."

Brit hid a smile. "We'll clean up the maze, and I'll be right down, Harrison." Loaded with the assortment of bats, gloves, and tennis shoes, she followed Murphy into his room.

Murphy set Tom back into the cage and stared glumly at the tiny creature.

"Perk up, Murphy," Brit said cheerfully as she put the toys where they belonged. "Tom's back home and safe."

"Yeah, but Dad's mad at me now. This has been a terrible day. Everything bad's happened."

Sensing Murphy's need to talk, Brit sat on the side of his bed. "What else went wrong today, Murphy?"

"Nothing." His small face was pinched tightly as he pretended to concentrate on Tom's cage.

"Gee, Murphy, everybody has a bad day now and then. Have you forgotten about your birthday next week? I'm already planning a party just for you."

"Really?"

"Sure. You get to pick whatever food you want for supper. What's your favorite kind of cake?"

"Chocolate. With chocolate icing."

"Okay, chocolate it is," Brit said with a grin. "What kind of presents do you want? I'd be glad to give your dad a few hints. Need a new bike? What about a stereo Walkman?"

"Naw, none of those." Murphy studied the mouse even more closely.

"You know, Murph, your birthday is special. Wishes come true when you blow out all the candles."

"Not my wish."

"It could," Brit said. "What's your wish?"

"If I had my real wish, I'd get a different name.

That's all I want. I hate Murphy." His voice cracked at the end, and Brit could tell he was desperately fighting tears.

"Oh, honey, I'm sorry. It's really a very special name for a special boy. Your mom and dad loved you very much and picked this name just for you."

"I don't like it! Nobody asked me what I thought about it."

"No, you were a little young," Brit said tenderly.

"It's a dumb name, and everybody teases me about it. Everybody at school and at home. Don't tell me some dumb town has the same name. I don't care. I hate it."

"Yes, I can see that. And I'm sorry I mentioned it."

"Brit! Ready to go?" Harrison called from downstairs.

"In a minute," she answered loudly, then turned back to Murphy. "What would you change your name to?"

"I don't know. Jeff, maybe. There are three Jeffs in my homeroom and nobody teases them."

"Wouldn't that get a little confusing to have four Jeffs in one homeroom?"

Murphy shrugged and scuffed one tennis shoe on the carpet.

"What about John? That's part of your real name, isn't it? And it's a pretty regular name."

Murphy studied the ceiling. "I guess John wouldn't be as bad as Murphy."

Harrison called again.

"Murphy, I have to go now," Brit said, and stood

126

to leave. "I'll see what I can do about your problem."

"Nothing, that's what."

"You never know," she said mysteriously. "You'd better keep Tom in his cage now. No more taking him out to pet him."

"How'd you know?"

Brit winked. "I know. I have brothers, and they always took their mice out to pet them. And the darned little things always got away."

Murph grinned guiltily at her.

Brit left wondering how in the world she would broach this sensitive subject with Harrison. However, she had to do something. Murphy was perfectly miserable, and Harrison should know about it.

At the foot of the stairs, Harrison offered her his arm. "You are one super mouse-catcher, lady. And you did it without getting a run in your stocking or wrinkling your dress. Ready to go—again? This time I'm pulling the plug on the phone. We'll probably be just in time for dessert."

She gripped his arm. "Actually, I've worked up quite an appetite crawling around on the floor. Mind if I stand beside the hors d'oeuvre table and stuff myself with chips and dip?"

"Not at all. As long as you're with me, I don't mind anything you do."

It was with a spirited sense of humor that they made it through the evening with influential congressmen and their wives. However, Brit's natural beauty outshone the array of furs and sparkling jewels.

127

On the way home, Harrison gazed at her admiringly. "You were charming, Brit. You dazzled them so much, they forgot we were an hour late."

"It isn't often that the Quintessential Woman is invited to such an impressive affair."

"This evening was very important to me, Brit. Thank you for coming."

"My pleasure." She paused as they pulled up to her apartment, hoping this was a good time to bring up Murphy's problem. "Uh, Harrison, I have something very important to discuss with you. A, uh, problem. Would you like to come in for a few minutes?"

"Of course," he said eagerly, and followed her inside.

She flipped on the lamp and motioned to the living room. "Have a seat. I'll get us some decaf."

When she returned with steaming cups, Harrison smiled. "Funny, I never pictured your place looking so—"

"Cluttered?" she asked brightly. "It's mostly Riley's stuff. She's a plant nut, and now that I'm at your house, I just let her have free rein around here."

"I see. Too busy keeping other people's places spotless."

"Something like that," she said, sipping her coffee and wondering just where to begin.

Harrison solved her dilemma. "What's your problem, Brit?"

"Well, it really isn't my problem. It's Murphy's."

"Oh, if it's about the birthday party, I'll go along

128

with whatever you want to do. Games, hats, cake, candles, the works. It's fine with me."

"No, it isn't exactly the party. It's far more serious than that."

Harrison looked curiously at her, waiting for her to continue.

"I'm not sure how to go about this diplomatically, Harrison, but I may as well just say it. Murphy is very unhappy with his name."

Harrison waved his hand. "Oh, that's just a phase. He'll get over it."

"No, I'm afraid he considers it very serious. And it seems to be getting worse."

"The teasing, you mean? I'll speak to Shane about it. You're right. I should put a stop to the teasing."

"It isn't just at home. The kids at school tease him, too. I'm afraid the teasing will only stop if his name is changed to something else. Something the kids can't tease about."

"What? Change his name? That's ridiculous."

"Well, I know it sounds extreme at first, but it was Murphy's idea. And I thought the birthday would be a good time to—"

"Wait a minute. You think we should actually go along with this foolish idea?"

"It isn't foolish to Murphy."

He rubbed his palm in frustration across his chin, muttering, "Damned craziest notion I've ever heard of!"

"I know how you must feel, Harrison," Brit murmured.

"No, you don't. Murphy is a special name to me.

He was a college buddy, and we were damned good friends through some pretty tough times."

"Oh, dear," she murmured sympathetically. "I tried to explain to Murphy that you thought the name was terrific, for a terrific kid."

"Well, that should settle it, because it's the truth."

"No, it doesn't settle anything, Harrison. Murph didn't care. Try to understand that the friend who means so much to you isn't the same to your son. Oh, God, that sounds awful." She struggled between loyalty for Harrison and her understanding of Murphy's feelings. "He told me that a different name is all he wants for his birthday."

"As a gift? I've never heard of such a crazy thing."

"Sure you have. People change their names all the time."

"But he's just a kid!"

"But he's a pretty big kid, big enough to make some decisions for himself."

"You sound like you're on his side."

Brit leaned forward earnestly. "You will be, too, when you realize how important this is to him, Harrison. I can only tell you that he asked me to intercede. And he had tears in his eyes. Now, you know for a kid his age to feel that adamantly about something, it has to be important."

Harrison glared, speechless, and she took that as an opening. "I've been thinking about it. Perhaps we could have a name-changing ceremony at his party next week. Something spiffy with candles and a clanging bell that shifts his name from Murphy to a more ordinary one."

"You already have this crazy thing planned?" Harrison rose and paced around the room.

"No, I don't have anything planned. I haven't mentioned any of this to Murphy, in case you think I'm working behind your back. I wanted to get your input, your suggestions."

"How about dropping the subject?"

"Harrison! I told you how important this is to him. I'm only thinking about Murphy with those big tears in his eyes. How would you feel about a name shift from his first to his middle name? We could call him John instead of Murphy."

"It'll be quite a change. What about Avery and Shane? What'll happen if they want to change their names? You simply aren't thinking straight, Brit."

She sighed and nodded. "I suppose I've been thinking only about Murphy. I'm sorry, Harrison. You're right. I've overlooked your feelings about this. But the way I see it, Murphy's just a kid, struggling to live with a nickname he despises. And his feelings really matter."

"I think that's a simplistic view." He headed for the door. "But I'll think about it."

"Harrison, don't take my word for it. Talk to Murphy. Please."

He nodded curtly. "Right. See you Sunday night."

Brit watched his Volvo pull away from the parking space with tears in her eyes. She felt like a rabbit trapped in the bottom of a deep hole, surrounded by darkness with no way out. No future, especially now, for her and Harrison.

But maybe, just maybe, Murphy had a chance to get his birthday wish.

Brit spent the weekend in worrying about the heated exchanges between Harrison and her. Had she been too forceful or not strong enough? He probably thought she was meddling and insensitive. With his curt nod of good-bye at her apartment door, there had been no overtures of making love. No subtle persuasion, no blatant insistence. Maybe their relationship—if you could call it that—was over.

That thought only instigated more worry. What would happen to Murphy? She could only hope Harrison would be gentle and understanding with the boy.

Brit was such dreary company that Riley finally insisted that they attend a Sunday afternoon movie. "There, now," she murmured dreamily on the way home. "Wasn't Robert Redford absolutely wonderful?"

"He was okay," Brit admitted.

"Okay? You *are* sick! Maybe you have a fever!"

"Knock it off, Riley," Brit grated, then lifted apologetic eyes to her friend. "Sorry. I didn't mean to snap."

"It's Harrison, isn't it?" Riley shook her head in dismay. "I knew it! He's just too good-looking to expect you to flit in and out of his house without a broken heart!"

"I interfered with a family matter. Murphy's

name. You can't really blame Harrison for being upset with me."

Riley gave her friend a sympathetic look. "You tried to do what you thought was right, Brit."

"Tell that to an almost-ten-year-old kid. And the worst of it is that I'll keep on and Harrison will keep on. But poor Murphy will still be stuck with a name he hates."

Riley nodded. "But you can't hold yourself responsible, Brit. You didn't name him. And you did all you could for somebody that's not even your own child."

On Sunday night, Brit quietly slipped back into her little downstairs room at the Kents'. She wondered what she would do if Harrison asked her to leave now. Sighing, she knew what she'd do. After all, she was only an employee. One who was in love not only with her employer but also with his kids.

A knock at her door set her heart pounding. When she opened it, she stared up into Harrison's brooding face. She forced a smile and tried to read his closed expression. "Hello, Harrison."

"Brit, uh . . . you were right. Murphy is damned serious about this name thing. We discussed it at great length this weekend and have come to an understanding."

"Oh?" She stiffened, thinking that Harrison had quelled the ten-year-old's name rebellion once and for all.

"Yes. We're going to change his name to John at the party. You and I can discuss the particulars later in the week." Harrison then wheeled around and headed for his workshop.

Brit stared after him, pressing her fingers to her lips. Large, grateful tears formed in her eyes. There was still hope, for Murphy and for her!

CHAPTER EIGHT

On the night of Murphy's tenth birthday, flickering candlelight cast lanky shadows into the corners of the Kent living room. Classical music swelled to a crescendo and faded away as the tall man in the center of the room raised both arms. Brit, Shane, and Avery gathered in a half-circle facing Harrison, who was resplendent in his black doctoral robes and tinfoil crown.

Gravely Harrison addressed the bathrobe-clad boy kneeling at his feet. "The Majestic Grand High Wizard of Antidisestablishmentarianism will now hear the petition from one of his subjects," he pronounced in sonorous tones.

Avery tugged on Brit's hand. "What's a petition?" she whispered.

"A request," Brit whispered back.

The little girl hopped up and down. "Then I petition to go to the bathroom."

"Can you wait?"

Avery jumped faster. "No-o-o."

Harrison's eyebrow rose a notch, and he glanced at Brit. "Is the assemblage ready to hear the petition?"

"Perhaps another short musical interlude would be appropriate, your Majestic Grand High Wizardship," Brit answered, turning up the sound on the stereo to drown out Shane's laughter. "One of your subjects has an urgent appointment."

Murphy looked pained. "She always has to go to the bathroom when something important is happening."

"I'll be right back," Avery called, racing up the stairs. "Don't petition without me, Murph."

"Jeez." Murphy sat back on his haunches in disgust.

"At least she won't be able to call you that much longer," Brit reminded him.

Murphy brightened. "Hey, that's right."

"I think this new name stuff is dumb." Shane lounged against the sofa. "How're we supposed to remember it?"

Harrison cast a warning glance at Shane. "It's not dumb, and you will remember."

"I dunno."

Avery hurtled down the stairs. "I'm back!"

"Okay, everyone take your places again," Brit instructed, turning off the music. "We can begin, your Wizardship."

Once again Harrison raised both arms. "The Majestic Grand High Wizard of Antidisestablishmentarianism will now hear the petition from one of his subjects. Proceed, vassal."

Murphy glanced up questioningly at the figure towering above him. "That's me?"

"Yes."

"Then I—I want to change my name to—to John," he stammered.

"The Majestic Grand High Wizard hears your request. He examines it from all aspects and finds it worthy. Your request is hereby"—Harrison paused dramatically—"granted."

"Oh, boy!" Murphy started to leap up but was restrained by a word from his father.

With calm precision Harrison raised a plastic sword and placed it alternately on each of the boy's shoulders. "By the authority vested in me as the Majestic Grand High Wizard of Antidisestablishmentarianism"—Harrison paused to glare at Shane, who was shaking with silent laughter—"I now pronounce you John Murphy Kent, hereafter to be known by all those present and absent as John."

A cheer went up from the assembled group.

"And let it be known," Harrison continued when the noise abated, "that anyone consistently addressing you by anything other than the aforementioned name of John will be immediately and summarily dealt with."

"What'll you do?" Shane asked, smirking. "Throw us in the dungeon?"

Harrison turned a baleful eye on his oldest son. "Shane, you don't want to find out the punishment for this crime. Don't test it."

Shane bravely tried to maintain his knowing smirk, but beneath his father's unwavering stare the boy's nonchalance faded. "Okay," he said quietly. "I'll call him John."

Harrison bent his head in acknowledgment and

137

returned his attention to the boy in front of him. "You may rise, John Murphy Kent."

Tears sprang to Brit's eyes at the expression of wonder on the boy's face as he stood up.

"You mean I'm really John?"

"That's right," Harrison replied.

The boy smiled beatifically. "Thanks, Dad."

"You're welcome, Mur—John."

Brit watched with a lump in her throat as father and son embraced. Harrison had come through like a champ once he'd become convinced that the name change was necessary.

He had planned the ceremony, which he and Brit agreed should take place during the birthday celebration. Harrison promised to handle the necessary legal paperwork later, after the robot was finished. In the meantime, tonight's ritual had taken care of the immediate problem within the family.

Avery pulled at her father's voluminous sleeve. "We all have to call him John instead of Murphy?"

"Yes, we do, Avery."

"But he's really still Murphy, right?"

Harrison squatted down and drew Avery onto his knee. "He's the same boy he's always been, but he has a different first name. One he likes better. It won't be easy to call him by his new name of John, but you're a smart girl. I know you can do it."

Avery poked her brother playfully in the stomach. "Hi, John," she said with a giggle.

The boy grinned. "That's me."

Brit stepped forward and held out her hand. "Congratulations, John."

"Thanks." He shook her hand solemnly and looked her straight in the eye. "I really mean it."

She squeezed his hand. "I know. Ready for cake and ice cream, birthday boy?"

"You bet!" The newly christened John tore off his bathrobe and raced to the dining room, followed closely by Shane and Avery.

Harrison pulled the crown from his head and began unhooking the heavy robe. "I wonder if John can pack away as much cake and ice cream as Murphy used to?" He gave Brit a sly wink.

"We're about to find out." Brit lowered her voice. "You were terrific, Harrison."

"Oh, yeah?" He glanced up and caught her gaze.

"Yeah," she said softly. "Mur—I mean John loved the ceremony. I did, too."

"A little corny, maybe."

"That's just what we needed. I—" Words of love hovered, ready to be spoken, but she didn't dare say them. "I appreciate all you've done. The games were inspired, and you even pretended to enjoy that horrible chili dog, although I couldn't finish mine."

He chuckled. "I guess you didn't see me slip half of it into my napkin. But Murphy—I mean John—devoured the meal."

"That's all that's important."

"You're right. You've been very wise about all this, Brit, and I'm grateful for your part in it, too." Behind the silver-rimmed glasses, his dark eyes grew warm with emotion. "And you look absolutely beautiful tonight," he whispered.

A thrill of pleasure and desire shot through her. Why had she been holding herself aloof from this wonderful man? The reasons seemed unimportant as she drank in the passion of his gaze. "Thank you."

"Thank you, lovely lady, for being here." His eyes glowed hot with desire. "That outfit is almost as sexy as the silver dress. I've never seen you in a flowered pattern before."

Brit glanced down at the silky tunic and pants. "Flowers usually aren't my style, but—"

"I disagree. Don't be afraid of the soft, feminine side of you, Brit. Is that material as touchable as it looks?" He reached over to finger the loose-hanging sleeve. "Mm. Nice."

Brit held perfectly still, but her heart was beating triple time. "Glad you like it."

"I can think of only one thing softer than this material." His fingers brushed gently up and down her arm beneath the sleeve. "I've been going crazy the last few days, Brit."

"Harrison, we—"

Shane called from the dining room, interrupting her. "Hey, is anybody gonna bring in the cake or should I?"

"I'll get it," Brit called back, and looked pleadingly at Harrison. "The children need me."

His voice was low and intense. "No more than I do."

"I can't—"

"Hush, my Quintessential Woman. Don't make any negative statements now. We'll talk later."

She didn't respond. Later. That meant after the kids were in bed, when the house was quiet and they

140

were all alone. The idea was very appealing—and very dangerous.

"Hey, Dad," Shane called again. "Want me to hook up the electronic match for the candles?"

"Sure, son."

Brit rolled her eyes. "Electronic match?"

Harrison grinned sheepishly. "Won't burn your fingers."

"Burning your fingers is part of the tradition, Harrison."

He shook his head ruefully and gave her an affectionate glance. "Shane," he called out, "forget the electronic match this time."

Brit propped the pillows against the headboard of her bed and picked up a business magazine. She thumbed it absently, hoping that reading would put her to sleep. Harrison had promised they would talk, but he'd provided no real opportunity to do so.

She couldn't fault him, though. Brit closed the magazine and recalled with fondness how Harrison had focused all his attention on Mur—John. Brit mentally corrected herself. She'd have to work hard to remember that Murphy was now John, but the effort would be well worth it.

After the kids were in bed, Brit had expected Harrison to appear in the kitchen where she was finishing the last of the cleanup. But he disappeared, probably to his workshop.

Brit told herself she was better off not being alone with Harrison, considering her present frame of mind. His tender regard for his children, especially the newly dubbed John, had chipped away at Brit's resolve to keep her distance.

If she had thought she loved him before, she was certain of it after tonight's celebration. But at this very moment, he was probably working on that infernal robot and had forgotten all about her. Damn that machine, anyway! She flipped open the magazine and tried once more to read.

The tap at her bedroom door was soft, but it reverberated in her brain like thunder. Could it possibly be Harrison at this hour? Surely not, but who else?

Brit pulled on her robe and fluffed her hair. Why had she taken off her makeup so soon? Too late now. But then, he'd seen her this way once before, when they had—no, she wouldn't think of that now. They would talk. Only talk, she repeated to herself as her heartbeat pounded in her ears.

When she opened the door and saw him standing there, all thoughts of talking fled. She gripped the doorknob fiercely to keep from opening her arms to him and giving away the rush of pleasure she felt when he smiled at her that way.

"What's all this?" She glanced at the paper bag he carried in one hand. He had a bottle under the other arm and held two goblets by their stems.

"I hope you like Chinese." He thrust the bag forward. "And I brought champagne to toast the name change."

"Food?" She glanced in confusion at the package he placed in her arms.

"I don't know about you, but half a chili dog and some barbecued chips don't fill me up. So I snuck out after the kids were asleep to buy us some real dinner."

Brit smiled. So he hadn't been working on the hated robot, after all. "How thoughtful of you."

"And I brought a real corkscrew for the champagne."

"Even more thoughtful."

"Well, may I come in?"

Brit couldn't think of a graceful way to turn aside such a considerate gesture as bringing her a decent supper. She stood aside and he walked into the bedroom, filling the small space, charging the air with anticipation. Brit knew the meal was a ploy, an excuse for them to be alone. But she hesitated only a fraction of a second before closing the door behind him.

"I don't have a table and chairs," she pointed out unnecessarily.

"The floor's fine." He sat down cross-legged and placed the bottle and glasses in front of him before taking off his shoes. "This is more fitting for Chinese food, anyway."

"True." As Brit sat across from him, she noticed how his position emphasized his muscled thighs— and more—and warmth rushed through her body. *Easy, Brit.* "The Far Eastern way is much simpler, I guess."

"In some things," Harrison agreed, working the cork carefully from the bottle. "But not when it comes to making love."

Brit flushed. "Are you speaking from personal experience?"

"No. I read a lot." The cork came out with pop.

"Oh." Her imagination went wild at the thought of Harrison reading about exotic lovemaking techniques. She tried to think of something bright and witty to say, but her tongue wasn't working very well.

As he gripped the bottle and poured both glasses full, she admired his arms with an erotic sprinkling of dark hair that emphasized his masculine appeal. She remembered how he had caressed her so knowingly during their passion-filled night in his room, and she began to tremble.

He handed her a goblet and raised his own. "To John Murphy Kent."

"And the father who loves him very much," Brit added, meeting Harrison's gaze as their glasses touched.

"Yes, I do." Slowly he brought the rim to his mouth and drank, but he never stopped looking at her.

She sipped the frothy liquid, enjoying how the tiny bubbles exploded against her lips and tongue. Harrison's touch was like that, she thought, like bursting bubbles of champagne against her skin.

He set his glass down on the rug beside him and smiled into her eyes, as if he could read her thoughts. "This is nice," he said gently.

"Yes."

"I suppose we should eat this food."

"Yes, I suppose we should."

With a reluctant sigh he turned his attention to the paper sack and began unloading the small cardboard cartons inside.

"Anything I can do to help?"

"Absolutely not. The Quintessential Woman deserves a rest once in a while. I'm providing this meal."

Brit laughed. "It is a treat to be waited on for a change."

"And no kids to worry about."

"No." She took another sip of champagne to calm her runaway excitement.

"Just you and me." The look he gave her was ablaze with the same emotions that clamored within her own body.

Her conscience told her sternly that she should put a stop to this cozy rendezvous—and fast. But his presence set off reactions she could no longer control, desires that demanded to be satisfied. One more night in his arms. How she longed for one more night!

"Just you and me," she repeated, taking another swallow of champagne.

"And five cartons of Chinese food," Harrison said with a wry smile. "Come on, here are your chopsticks."

"I don't know how to use them," she protested with a chuckle.

"Great. This will be exactly like in the movies. I'll feed you. Now stop laughing and open up."

"You'll do no such thing, you crazy man. I'm not some baby sparrow."

"Open up before this shrimp drops in your lovable lap."

Brit looked cross-eyed at the pink morsel caught between the wooden prongs being jabbed in the direction of her mouth. "Oh, all right, but this is ridiculous." She opened her mouth, and Harrison popped the shrimp in with practiced ease. It tasted delicious, and she smiled at him. "More."

"I knew it. The woman's voracious." He caught a bit of pineapple between the chopsticks and laid it on her tongue. Then he picked up a chunk of green pepper and put it in his own mouth.

Brit found the experience of being fed and sharing the same utensils highly sensuous. With a little coaxing from Harrison, she agreed to maneuver the chopsticks herself and feed him.

"I'll make this a real challenge," he said. "We'll keep score. Every neat bite with no fallout is a point."

"No fair. You already know how."

"I'll give myself a handicap." He took off his glasses and reached back to put them on her dressing table.

"Terrific! I'm a cinch to win now." She loved taunting him, loved the supercharged atmosphere that sizzled between them as they played.

"Don't be so sure, Brit. I think I could find that luscious mouth of yours blindfolded."

Her lips tingled as she remembered the magic of his kiss. "We'll see," she said in an unsteady voice.

Harrison's boast proved correct as he unerringly directed the food to her open mouth. She, on the other hand, dropped numerous tidbits and scored almost no points.

"I'm going to starve to death, woman!" he complained.

"No, you won't. I'll take care of this." Laughing with giddy abandon, she began scooping the dropped food from his lap and putting it in his mouth. Her fingers tingled with the unrestrained excitement of touching him at last, supposedly in fun.

"Hey, no fair!" He caught her wrists. "Brit, you can't—" He fell silent as they stared, each recognizing the look of raw passion in the other's eyes. "Brit," he groaned, crushing her to him and seeking the lips that parted eagerly under his.

With a deep sigh she accepted the demanding pressure of his mouth, the familiar roughness of his chin. She opened willingly to invite the firm thrust of his tongue, and his name was a continuous chant in her mind as he stroked the moist inner recesses with deliberate purpose. Harrison. How she wanted this man, this tender, considerate, crazy man.

His arms wound around her, guiding her upward as he brought them both to a kneeling position. Untying her robe, he let it fall open and pulled her close. Brit delighted in pressing herself against his broad chest, his strong thighs, his throbbing masculinity. She gloried in his moan of pleasure as she rubbed suggestively against him.

With one hand she caressed the nape of his neck; with the other she fumbled with the buttons of his shirt and ran her palm sensuously across the nipples buried in swirls of dark hair. He shuddered and pushed her robe down over her shoulders until it fell in a heap between them.

As he fingered the silken straps of her nightgown, he lifted his head and chuckled raggedly. "Where's my favorite nightshirt?"

"Gone," she whispered, kissing the hollow of his throat. Ever since the first night he had made love to her, Brit had put away her nightshirts and worn a filmy gown to bed. She had refused to admit to herself the reason—that she had hoped some night to be back in Harrison's arms.

"You'd better not have thrown it away."

"No."

"That's good. It has sentimental value."

"It's a silly old shirt I want to forget," she insisted, running the tip of her tongue along the prickly ridge of his jaw.

"I could never forget it, or how you looked—your cheeks flushed, your hair tousled, and your beautiful body gift-wrapped in that unbelievable nightshirt." He framed her face in both hands. "No matter how bad my day has been or how discouraged I become, I can conjure up that picture of you and the world is a wonderful place again."

She gazed at him with shining eyes. "I'm glad."

"Of course, that mental picture also brings on some other reactions." His hands slid slowly down her neck to her shoulders and pushed the straps free. "Because my next image is this." He drew the nightgown down to her waist. "Stand up, Brit," he urged gently.

When she obeyed, he pulled the gown to her feet. His breathing grew labored as his hands skimmed up the backs of her legs. "God, how I want you," he whispered. Cupping her firm behind, he pressed her forward and kissed the sensitive indentation of her navel.

Her trembling fingers raked through his thick hair as he moved lower, trailing kisses to the quivering center of her. She gasped as his intimate caress became ever bolder. "I want you, too," she moaned. Her legs grew weak as he built the spiraling tension within her, and just when she thought she would fall, he stood up and swept her into his arms.

He laid her on the bed and tugged off his own clothes. "See what you do to me?" he said, his chest heaving. "You're driving me insane, traipsing around this house and not allowing me to touch you. By God, you'll know I've touched you this time. I want you to be a little crazy, too."

"I already am," she pleaded.

His eyes were dark coals as he came to her. His ravenous kisses began at her mouth, but they were soon consuming every inch of her until she was writhing against the tangled sheets.

"Did you learn this—from books?" she asked, panting.

"No," he murmured, finding yet another sensitive spot on her heated body, "instinct. You bring out something primitive in me, Brit."

"I—oh! Yes, Harrison. There! Please . . ." she begged. "Now, please . . ."

"Yes, now," he groaned. He grasped her hips and lifted her to meet the hungry thrust of his manhood. A cry escaped his lips as he sank into her silken depths. He'd thought he might never again feel this rapture, but here she was, enfolding him, welcoming him.

"Don't forget," he urged against her ear. "Don't forget how this feels."

"I couldn't . . . oh, Harrison!" Her fingers dug into his shoulders.

"Don't forget," he repeated, his breathing harsh

against her throat as he increased the tempo, taking them both closer, closer. "Not ever . . . my God, Brit!" He surged forward, and she rose with him as they exploded together.

And she knew as she floated weightlessly on their shared cloud of fulfillment that she would never, never forget.

CHAPTER NINE

The morning sun filtered through the blinds and created pale arrows of light across the bed.

His touch was gentle, soothing, unmistakably seductive. He stroked her hair, pushing it back from her face, and his warm breath softly brushed her skin. A single finger traced the curve of her lips, the slope of her cheek, the curl of her ear. Then his lips followed, breathing hot, sexy words between kisses.

She stirred, unable to ignore his erotic advances, incapable of halting the slow rekindling of sensuous fires. A small flame flickered from her center and radiated outward in all directions. Once again she was alive with desire. Turning her face toward him, Brit caught his evocative fragrance, musky and very masculine. *Nice—and sexy,* she thought, smiling.

"Sorry to wake you," he whispered in a voice so low it sounded like a bass rumble coming from his chest. "I have to leave you soon, and I couldn't resist touching you one more time."

"What a marvelous wake-up call," she murmured, taking in a deep breath. His strong essence seemed to fill her body with longing and revitalization. She wanted more of him and nuzzled his neck playfully. "I wish we could stay here like this all morning."

"All day," he murmured, kissing her pulsing temple. His arm slid beneath her head, drawing them closer. "I wish we could stay like this forever, Brit."

Pressing her ear to his chest, she felt the vibrations of his heart pounding through her. She tried to attune her own body to his by altering her breathing to match his and willing her heart to accompany his beat. "Yes, forever," she murmured. But instinctively a small part of her knew this paradise with Harrison couldn't last forever.

"Now is forever, Brit. This moment is all we have." His hand skimmed over the length of her back, stroking the silkiness of her skin. He pressed against her lower back and cupped the curve of her buttocks. "You feel so good next to me. So smooth and soft in the right places."

"Oh, Harrison, hold me. Just like this." She matched her slender feminine shape to his hard male form. She marveled at the magnificence of his tautening maleness, asserting itself insistently against her thigh.

"Brit, ah, Brit, you're wonderful. See what you do to me? I want you all hours of the day and night."

She snuggled closer, moving sensuously between the vise of his thighs. He was like velvet steel, strong and virile and aroused. She found it wildly erotic, just lying there with him like that. "Me, too. You're the most exciting man I've ever known, Harrison."

"Excitable, you mean," he teased, and kissed a

hot path to each throbbing breast. "I can't be this close to you without touching."

"Electrifying," she added with a small laugh as his lips closed over each tight nipple, first one and then the other. She wriggled with delight as his lips tugged gently and her breasts swelled to plump, creamy globes.

"You're beautiful, you know, Brit. I love to see you respond in my hands like this."

"I love what your hands do to me, Harrison. Love your touch." Then she caught her lip between her teeth. What were they saying here? Waltzing all around love statements yet not saying them. Not admitting a love that was definitely there. What exactly were they feeling besides a spontaneous and glorious lust for each other?

Oh, yes, his hands did wonderful things to her, made her feel as no others had, made her risk everything for the joy of being in his arms. Pushing aside her reservations, Brit lifted her mouth to meet his kiss and eagerly parted her lips for the possessive invasion of his tongue.

His sensuous touches didn't stop. Strong hands traveled the length of her body, admiring every soft, feminine curve, exploring each hidden pleasure. And when she writhed beneath the pressure of his probing fingers, Brit whimpered, "Don't wait any longer. Oh, Harrison."

"Come to me, my darling Brit," he whispered, and pulled her over him.

Enthusiastically she straddled his hips, massaging his chest with hungry hands. Oh, how she loved to touch him! She stretched herself over him, kissing

153

his lips and neck and chest. Her tongue roamed through the feathery hairs, tasting the pungency of his skin.

With an upward thrust of his hips, he moaned, "Ah, Brit, come on, my darling. Don't torment me like this. I want you."

She smiled and teased his body a moment longer before lowering herself over him. With obvious feminine delight she forged them together, slowly and surely, until he filled her completely. "And I want you," she said, squirming with pleasure.

He stroked her hips, his large hands guiding her actions firmly. "Now, Brit."

Purring with pleasure, she murmured, "You're mine, Harrison Kent. All mine." The words caught in her throat—how she wished she could believe them! Wished she could claim him outside this room and shout to the world, "He's mine!"

Together they rode to the crest of ecstasy, moving in unison. Her fair skin contrasted with his darkness as the two joined in a single rhythm. An ultimate fury of excitement and emotion carried them over the brink, and Brit cried out for joy, shuddering repeatedly until she slumped over him in exhaustion.

"Oh, God, Harrison, I love you," she mumbled from kiss-swollen lips.

They lay there quietly for a long time. Brit felt his heart pounding through her, and her own heart sang with love for the man beneath her. Unable to restrain her feelings any longer, she had acknowledged her love to him.

Yet Harrison had not answered. He hadn't responded.

Brit hadn't been able to hold back, even knowing she was setting herself up for the fall of her life. No, not just a fall. A crash.

The room was silent. Eventually a long sigh escaped from deep within Harrison's chest, and they both knew it signaled an end to this ecstasy they shared.

Brit shifted and lay facing away from him. "You don't have to say anything, Harrison. I just want you to know how I feel. I love you and care very much for your family. I know this complicates things, and obviously you don't—"

"It isn't that, Brit. Surely you must realize I care for you, too. Why, you're the first woman since Pam I've ever wanted to continue a relationship with."

"You mean I'm the only one you wanted to go to bed with for a second time, don't you?" Brit squeezed her eyes shut in agony. "Please don't compare me with your wife, Harrison. I'd never measure up to martyrdom."

"That's not true, Brit." His hand gripped her bare shoulder, and she quivered beneath his fingers. "You're the most beautiful, lovable woman I've ever met. And you can measure up to anyone. But I—I just feel it's too soon to really know about something as serious as love. Too soon for you to know, Brit. You might be infatuated with me. Maybe I'm infatuated, too." He rose from the bed and silently pulled his clothes over his lean brown body.

Brit kept her eyes averted. How could she face him now that she'd revealed her own deepest feelings? And he hadn't. She disagreed with his objections. It wasn't too soon for her to know if she loved him. And she wasn't merely infatuated. Her heart had defied her usual common sense and basic principles to fall in love with him.

When he was completely dressed, Harrison came over to the bed and sat on the edge. Gently he caressed her hair, then bent down and kissed her. She didn't turn away. His lips met hers tenderly, sweetly pairing with hers to express the depths of feelings he couldn't admit. And she accepted the only token he was willing to give her—his kiss, his body. Perhaps she should be grateful for that much.

But deep in her heart, Brit knew she had to have more. She had to have an admission, a commitment, from him. Otherwise she was throwing away her love.

Without another word, he left her room.

Brit stared at the closed door for long, agonizing minutes. She blinked furiously, but the tears came anyway. Dashing them away, she hurled herself into the bathroom for a shower.

She knew what she had to do. Perhaps she'd known all along, since the first time she ever saw him sexily draped in that towel. Tall, dark, masculine—and playing right into her wily little hands.

But not anymore.

Now she was in over her head with Harrison Kent and his rambunctious kids. She stepped into the shower and let it pepper her hard and hot.

The time to get out was now! She scrubbed her flesh vigorously with the decision. Yes, she had to leave. And the sooner the better.

Harrison failed to appear at breakfast, but the kids didn't seem to notice. They were too busy chattering away, merrily trying out John's new name.

"John John John," Avery chanted. "Not Murphy anymore."

"Please pass the butter, John," Shane giggled.

Brit placed more toast on the table and grinned at the happy boy. "I think you look taller today, John. You must have grown half an inch during the night."

He beamed with pride at the notion. "Ah, you can't grow at night, Brit."

"Sure you can," she said. "What else do you think your body's doing all night long while you're asleep? It doesn't want to disturb you with all that stretching."

Avery giggled delightedly and extended her arms upward. "Like this?"

"Yep." Brit nodded and hurried them through breakfast, trying not to think of her decision to leave. Or how she would tell them. "Come on, now, kids, it's almost time to catch the bus."

John approached her with a pencil and paper. "Would you write a note to my teacher, Brit? And explain, uh, you know, about my new name."

"Sure," Brit agreed, taking the pencil. Then she paused. "Maybe your dad should be the one to do this, John."

He shook his head. "Naw, he's too busy to bother. You do it, Brit."

"Why, honey, he's never too busy for you," Brit objected vehemently, trying to convince herself as well as John.

157

"Yes, he is. And you're always here. So please, Brit. That way they can start calling me by my real name today. It's important, Brit. Please!"

She looked at the sincerity in the young boy's face and couldn't deny him. "Well, all right. I guess I can do this much. But I'll tell your dad to call the teacher later for a better explanation."

"Okay." John hopped excitedly from one foot to the other while Brit scribbled a brief note.

When the three children left for school, Brit watched sadly as they disappeared down the street. How could she tell them she had to leave because she loved their father too much? It didn't make sense.

She wavered. Maybe she should stay. How could she possibly leave Harrison and these precious kids? And yet she knew she must.

Later Brit was in the process of finishing a comprehensive schedule for the Kent household on her portable computer when Harrison knocked on her door. "Brit? Sorry to interrupt, but this is important."

Rising, she plastered a bland expression on her face. She was determined not to show her true feelings. Not anymore. It left her too open to pain.

With hands propped on slim blue-jeaned hips, he grinned jauntily. "I feel like celebrating today. Let's go out for lunch."

"Celebrating? What?" Brit couldn't imagine that this day had anything to celebrate.

"I've finished the robot. It's done, Brit!" Spontaneously he grabbed her shoulders and squeezed. "I can't tell you how I'm feeling right now. The elation! The pride! The expectations I have for it! I knew you'd want to share this with me."

She almost staggered back. "I—oh, yes, congratulations. I'd like to go with you, Harrison, but I can't possibly. Too much to do."

He motioned impatiently. "Do it later. This is something just for us. There's no one I'd rather share this joy with, Brit. You understand what I've been through to accomplish this. Only you understand me."

"I'm p-proud of you, Harrison, but I don't have time."

"Then maybe something simple like a picnic at Wolf Trap?"

She rubbed one arm nervously. "No, Harrison. You don't understand—"

"If it's what we talked about this morning, I want to assure you, I certainly do care about you. A lot."

"I'm sorry, Harrison," Brit rasped. "That isn't enough for me. I need more. And I'm afraid you can't give me what I want. What I need."

He looked at her in exasperation. "Like what?"

She lifted her chin. "Like a commitment."

"I told you I can't do that yet. But given time, who knows what—"

"I can't hang around until the mood strikes you, Harrison."

"What? You can't leave! We need you, Brit."

"Not really. I have your organization chart here. Anyone could come in and follow this plan. Or you and the kids can do it yourselves with a little effort."

"My God, Brit! This is crazy!"

"No, it isn't. It's self-defense. I'm all alone here,

Harrison. And I think I know why you don't want to commit yourself. You have your kids. And possibly a lingering love for Pam. Your work occupies every other corner of your life. You aren't ready for anything stronger than that. So you see, I do understand."

He glared at her, his mind whirling furiously. He had to do something to buy some time, to hold on to her a little longer. Oh, why the hell couldn't he tell her how he felt? How *did* he feel? "Will you, uh," he stammered, "stay with me—us—through this weekend? I need you, Brit. With the robot finished, I want to have another dinner for the financial backers. To demonstrate its complete abilities. The rest of the monies will be available after this, for marketing and publicity."

She blinked. "You want me to have another dinner for you?"

"I'd like you to be my hostess," he said with growing enthusiasm. "Why, if it weren't for you, I never would have finished it so soon. I owe you everything that has to do with this project, Brit. Plus you took care of my children so beautifully, with such warmth and love, I want to give you credit."

Brit's heart began to palpitate. *She* was responsible for his success? How absolutely absurd! She'd come here to sabotage his efforts, and instead she'd abetted them! "I certainly don't deserve credit, Harrison." She swallowed hard and tried to gather her wits. "That—that's not true!"

"Oh, don't be so modest, Brit."

"I mean it, Harrison. I don't want anything more to do with this project."

He shrugged. "Okay, whatever you say. But you and I know the truth. You've been invaluable to me, Brit. And to the kids. Why, just look how you took care of Shane's broken arm. And quieted Avery the night of the storm. And solved Murphy's name problem."

She nodded bleakly. "John."

"Yes, John," he amended. "We all need you, Brit."

"Please don't say that, Harrison."

"Say you'll stay, Brit."

She tried to breathe calmly and think this through. If she stayed until Friday night, she could see the robot perform. After all, that was her goal— to see it to completion. It would also give her time to tell the kids about her need to leave. "Maybe I could—"

"Then you'll stay?"

She drew herself up and thought of one thing. Here was her chance to see the robot's full demonstration. This was why she had come here in the first place, not to fall in love with the inventor. If she could put her emotions on hold for one more evening, she could see what he'd created to destroy her business. "Okay. I'll stay long enough to do the dinner."

"Great!" He grabbed her shoulders and kissed her lips soundly, then departed quickly.

Brit stared openmouthed, wondering why in the world she'd agreed. What was happening to her, anyway? Her emotions were a mess. One minute she

161

was adamant about leaving. The next, she was willing to stay a little longer. What did she really want to do?

For the first time in her life, Brit was undecided about herself, her feelings, her directions. And that was very much unlike her. She didn't like this waffling, incapable jellyfish she'd become. But she seemed unable to do anything about it.

As she set the dining-room table with china and crystal for dinner Friday night, Brit kept telling herself she was here tonight specifically to see the robot perform. It was her nemesis, and she had to know what it could do. That's why she was here, just for the robot. Oh, how she hated the mechanical thing! How she'd love to jerk a few wires loose!

When she finished, Brit stood back and admired her handiwork. Sparkling clean this time, with a floral centerpiece on the table, the entire room looked quite grand, even if she said so herself. With a sad smile she remembered the night John's mouse escaped and Mrs. Weeples had sat in the middle of the dining-room table screeching. Harrison had made a special effort to calm the lady; then he'd exhibited extraordinary fatherly patience as he crawled around on the floor in his dinner suit to catch the tiny beast.

But then, Harrison was an extraordinary man.

That was the night she'd learned the extent to which John hated his name. Who would he tell such intimate yearnings to when she left? She could only hope he'd go to Harrison in the future.

She had to stop thinking such thoughts. It was

162

over, and the sooner she admitted it and left, the better off they all would be.

Brit peered into the kitchen, where her French chef was preparing dinner. "Phillipe, are you sure Sir Wilfred will be here in time to serve? The guests should start arriving in about an hour."

"Oui, mademoiselle. He is never late."

Brit checked her watch. "I know, but I'd feel better if he were already here."

"Relax, mademoiselle." Phillipe gave Brit a fatherly gaze. "You seem, how you say, uptight about this dinner tonight. But do not worry. Sir Wilfred and I are a team."

"Oh, I'm not worried about your part, Phillipe," Brit objected quickly. "I know how capable you and Sir Wilfred are. It's just that I want this evening to go well." She was a quivering bowl of jelly inside, and it had nothing to do with the dinner. It had to do with the family she planned to leave.

Phillipe smiled reassuringly and readjusted his tall chef's hat. "Everything will be fine for this dinner, as long as you keep those—those crazy machines away from me!"

Brit laughed. "Oh you mean the Goody-Grabber and Cork-Torque and all the other kitchen gadgets? Don't worry. They're tucked away in the bottom cabinet."

"No more grabbing and poking by nosy machines for Phillipe," the Frenchman admonished, flexing one hand at her. "There is nothing like the human hand for a light touch."

Brit nodded appreciatively. "You know, I think

you're right, Phillipe. There's nothing quite like the hand for touching.''

Harrison appeared in the kitchen doorway, looking as anxious as a young boy with a valentine for his first sweetheart. "Would you like to see my brainchild?" he asked haltingly.

"What?" Brit's brow furrowed. "Oh, you mean—"

He nodded. "The multidigital latitudinarian scope robot. I need to bring it upstairs, and I thought you'd like a little preview demonstration."

Brit hesitated. Here was the moment she'd anticipated for weeks. And yet she was reluctant. Maybe she was afraid the robot would be too good, too perfect, too wonderful a creation. What she wanted to do was rip the precious brainchild apart! She forced a smile. "Why sure, Harrison."

"Come on, then," he said, leading the way to his workshop. With a grand motion, he threw open the door and pushed a few buttons on a hand-held control box.

The thing started climbing the stairs, clanking and heaving in a clumsy amble. Brit gaped at the five-foot-tall metal creature. "You're very clever," Brit mumbled as she watched the robot shift gaits and proceed in a rolling motion when it reached the top of the stairs.

Harrison pushed a few buttons, and the robot began vacuuming the floor. And without bumping into anything like the old one did. Once it halted, and a strange-looking hand lifted a stray sock from behind a chair. Harrison grabbed the sock with a satisfied laugh. "Aha! The scanner works perfectly! She can detect things we can't even see."

"She?" Brit watched in a blue-eyed daze. "She's an amazing woman." The damned thing seemed to be able to do everything a human did and even see things that were invisible to a normal eye. It was better than she had ever dreamed. Or worse! "She's like a wireless Wonder Woman, Harrison," Brit mumbled as she followed the incredible creature and her inventor.

"Wonder Woman . . . Wonder Woman! That's a great name for her, Brit. I think that's what I'll call her, at least for now." Harrison smiled. "Good idea! Very appropriate."

Brit gazed at him bleakly. Oh, this was just great. Not only had she enabled Harrison to build it, now she had even named her nemesis. Why couldn't she keep her mouth shut? "Wonder Woman is a little dated, don't you think? What about Megawoman?"

Harrison considered them for a moment. "I think Wonder Woman is timeless. And we all know about her. Still, Megawoman is new and sounds more contemporary. Either one is better than multidigital latitudinarian scope robot."

"Granted," Brit conceded with a grim smile, and watched the wireless wonder approach the kitchen.

The metal female halted before Phillipe and spoke in a sing-song tone, "Good evening. How may I serve you?"

"Oh oh oh!" Phillipe moaned, and hopped away from the amiable alien. *"Sacré bleu!* The ones from Mars have landed! We are taken!"

Despite her distress, Brit couldn't help laughing

with Harrison at the chef's startled reaction. "Meet Mr. Kent's newest robot, Phillipe, not an alien."

The pudgy gray-haired chef grabbed at his heart. *"Sacré bleu!* Please, do not scare Phillipe like this. You said all the crazy machines were hidden away."

"But this one's different, Phillipe," Harrison said, stepping forward. "This robot can do everything. It incorporates all the technology I have developed so far into one entity that can do anything. Just wait'll you see her tricks."

"Tricks?" Phillipe looked skeptically at the metal creature.

"Sure, just name it. All we have to do is set the program." Harrison held out the palm-size multidigital control for his perusal. "How would you like help stirring your sauce? Simply push a couple of buttons, and she'll hold the spoon and stir. Like so." Wonder Woman grasped a long-handled spoon and dipped into the creamy sauce on the stove.

Phillipe folded his arms over his ample belly. "I see this trick. But any monkey can stir. Have this square lady taste the sauce and tell me if it has enough flavor or if it needs more sugar."

Harrison looked at Phillipe with a rueful grin. "Okay, so she can't taste, Phillipe."

Phillipe's eyes narrowed. "I see. Even a monkey can taste and let you know if the sauce is good or not. There is nothing like a mouth for tasting, monsieur."

"But a monkey needs food and care. Wonder Woman just sits in the corner, waiting for your command," Harrison said.

"Then let this Wonder Woman stay in the corner

until I give the command!" Phillipe countered, and waved both hands frantically. "Please, get her out of the kitchen! As long as I have two hands and a mouth, monsieur, I will do my own cooking, without help from a tin woman with an armored bosom!"

"She's made of stainless steel," Harrison grated, and pushed a few buttons. Wonder Woman deposited the spoon onto the stove and found her spot in the corner. Brit hid a grin as Harrison glared at the French chef. And Phillipe glared back.

"I'm leaving her here while I go to get dressed," Harrison said to Brit. "After dinner, she'll have an opportunity to perform for an audience that appreciates her for what she is: a multidigital latitudinarian scope robot, soon to be known in the commercial world as Wonder Woman." He paused to glance at Phillipe. "You don't mind if Wonder Woman watches from the corner, do you?"

"Not at all, monsieur," Phillipe answered graciously. "She may learn something."

"L-learn? She already has the potential—" Harrison halted with a sigh and tossed his hands up before stalking out, muttering, "Impossible."

Brit kept an eye on Wonder Woman all evening. She understood Phillipe's distrust of the wonderful robot, but her own feelings were far deeper. They bordered on hatred.

Yet she realized that Wonder Woman was an amazing, innovative creation that indeed had the potential to replace the Quintessential Woman. Like any computer, the extent of her abilities depended on the operator. But the potential was there.

Brit knew that with very little effort she could do some sort of damage to the robot. Pulling a few wires wasn't entirely impossible. And the way Phillipe felt about the creature, he would gladly help. Or at the very least keep quiet about it.

Brit halted before Wonder Woman and examined her closely. Perhaps there was a vulnerable place somewhere. Carefully she pulled a lever, and a window on the back of the robot's head opened up. There a multitude of wires were exposed. All she had to do was—

Brit's hand reached out for those wires. Here was her chance to eliminate the major threat to her business, the chance she'd been hoping for since the day she had worked her way into Harrison's house.

But something made her stop.

This metal creature was Harrison's pride and joy —his work, his life. He'd poured years of research and thousands of hours of work into making this robot. Now he was almost ready to show the world what he had done, to make his contribution to mankind. And she, in a selfish act, wanted to destroy it.

What would Harrison think if he knew how she felt? If he could see her now? Oh, dear God, how could she do it?

Her hand froze.

Brit couldn't hurt him like that.

She withdrew her shaky hand and flipped the switch that closed the window on the robot's head. Heart pounding so that she could hardly breathe, Brit turned away.

Sir Wilfred sailed through the door and announced stiffly, "I suppose he doesn't need me anymore, madame. He said something about getting Wonder Woman. Is that you, Miss McIver?"

"No," Brit said sadly, and pointed to the corner. "It's her."

Sir Wilfred, Phillipe, and Brit hovered together and watched through the louvered doors to the dining room. Wonder Woman flawlessly performed her duties for the guests. She vacuumed, removed dishes from the table, even poured and served after-dinner coffee and brandy. Oh, yes, she certainly was efficient. As Harrison claimed, she could do everything.

Except taste, Phillipe had pointed out.

And love, Brit added mentally as she watched the incredible invention respond to Harrison's every command. She has no heart, Brit decided, and she can't love. Not like I can. But obviously Harrison doesn't need my love. He only needs Wonder Woman to be successful. And it certainly looks as if she is.

Brit had completed her job and had done it well. But now it was over, finished. And so was her life with Harrison. She was no longer needed; her love was not even recognized. With a heavy sigh, she disappeared to finish packing.

CHAPTER TEN

"Brit, are you in there?" Harrison's voice was urgent as he rapped on her bedroom door late that same night.

"Just a second," she replied wearily, snapping the latch on her suitcase. She'd also closed up the portable computer after filling its memory bank earlier in the evening with notes on the strengths and weaknesses of Harrison's robot. With that information she could plan an advertising campaign that might counteract the robot's appeal when it appeared on the market. Then again, maybe nothing would be able to stop the success of Wonder Woman.

"Brit! I need to talk to you."

With a sigh Brit walked to the door and flung it open. Still in his tuxedo, Harrison raised a bottle of champagne and two glasses. "Join me in a toast? They loved the robot. With their financial backing, Wonder Woman could be on the market in a year, bringing in royalties and . . ." He paused to glance at the suitcase on her bed. "Wait a minute, Brit. Surely you're not—"

She avoided his gaze, afraid he could tell she'd

been crying. "You knew I planned to leave after the robot was finished. I told you."

"No." He set the glasses and champagne on her dressing table. "You may have said it, but I didn't think you were really serious." He stepped closer and gently grasped her shoulders. "Come on," he coaxed with a smile. "We can talk this out. You don't have to rush away into the dark of night like this."

She stared at the floor. "Yes, I'm afraid I do."

"Aren't you being a little melodramatic? You and I should be celebrating, not fighting. Tonight was the culmination of all our hard work, and we deserve to crow a little." He tilted her chin up with one finger. "After all, we accomplished this triumph together, Brit."

Her vision blurred as she looked into his dark eyes. "That's the funny part," she said hoarsely. "Want to hear a good joke?"

"You've been crying," he murmured, touching his lips to her swollen eyelids.

"Tears of laughter," she lied, twisting away from him. She didn't want his tenderness now, not unless it was prompted by love. Spoken love. Love shouted from the rooftops. Damn him, anyway!

"I don't see anything to laugh about." His tender smile faded and his mouth compressed into a tense and angry line. "Not with your suitcase packed and ready to go. A few weeks ago you appeared like an answer to my prayers. We joined forces, and everything worked out beautifully. Why do you insist on ruining everything now?"

Brit wrapped her arms around her trembling

body. "Tell me, Harrison, did you ever stop to wonder why I showed up on your doorstep at that particular time?"

"Some promotion or other for your business." He waved one hand impatiently. "It doesn't matter why you were there. We were all damned lucky you agreed to help run the household."

She faced him and lifted her chin with a false sense of bravado. He might as well know the truth. "I wasn't on your doorstep by accident, Harrison. I deliberately planned to work my way into your household as a—a spy."

He began to laugh in disbelief and then his eyes narrowed behind the silver frames. "Just what do you mean by that?"

"I had to find out about your new robot."

Harrison took a menacing step forward, and his voice was dangerously calm. "If you're trying to say that some robotics firm hired you to steal my plans—"

"No." She stood her ground, although the taut coil of his body made her quiver with dread. She'd never felt the full force of his anger. She knew that he wouldn't hurt her physically, but even a verbal assault would be wrenching coming from the man she loved.

"Tell me about it, Brit," he said quietly.

"I needed information concerning the robot for myself, for my business. When I saw you on television, I knew your invention had the potential to jeopardize the Quintessential Woman. I recognized the appeal—people might prefer making a one-time

172

purchase of your robot instead of contracting for human household help."

Harrison's eyes darkened until they looked as hard as chips of ebony. "You're quite an actress, Brit McIver. Truly a Quintessential Woman. I knew what I paid you wasn't enough for all the time you devoted to this family, but I kidded myself that you did the extra work because you cared about the kids —about me."

"I did! I do," she amended quickly. "I'm trying to tell you how this whole thing got started. I began working for you in my own self-interest, but then I found out what neat kids you have. They've stolen my heart, Harrison." Her lower lip trembled. "Leaving them hurts. It hurts a lot." She caught her lip between her teeth to keep from breaking down again.

He made a half-motion toward her, then checked himself and shoved his hands in his pockets. To keep from looking at her he fixed his attention on a painting on the wall behind her. "Brit . . . I have to ask. Did you go to bed with me because you thought I might—I don't know—reveal secrets in my sleep or something?"

"Good God, no!" She glanced up in horror and was jolted by the misery reflected in his eyes. Her voice shook with emotion. "Harrison, you know how I feel. I should never have told you the other morning, but then I've made lots of mistakes recently."

He nodded slowly but still didn't look at her. "We've both made our share of mistakes." He walked over to the bed and sat down. Clasping his hands loosely between his knees, he bent his head in thought.

Brit caught herself reaching to stroke his thick, luxurious hair and abruptly pulled her hand back. She realized that he didn't want her comfort now, after she'd forced him to see that they were in competition, that they were enemies. Her admission of duplicity must have quenched any spark of love he might have felt.

Harrison sighed heavily and looked up. "Did you get the information you needed?"

She flushed. "I typed some notes into the computer tonight after I saw all the things the robot can do."

"Do you have any questions? I'd be glad to tell you anything you want to know."

"Why—why would you do that?"

His expression was bleak. "Because it doesn't matter. Not now."

"I don't understand."

"The robot is finished, Brit. The patent is filed, and production will begin very soon. I hadn't thought about how Wonder Woman might affect your business, but she probably will. I regret that, but it's inevitable. The information you've gained won't be of much use to you."

Brit recoiled at his arrogance. How dare he be so sure of that mechanical monster! "That's where you're wrong, Harrison. You may have a wonderful robot, but you don't know beans about marketing. I'll come up with an advertising campaign for the Quintessential Woman that will make Wonder Woman go dead in the water."

174

He shook his head. "I doubt it. Robotics are the future, whether you admit that fact or not. You may win a few skirmishes in this struggle against progress, but you'll lose the war, Brit."

"We'll see about that," she said through clenched teeth.

"Don't be so damned stubborn," he fumed, standing and walking toward her. "Face facts for a change."

"There's more to life than facts," she insisted, trying not to be intimidated by the masculine appeal that still drew her and made her want to fling herself into his arms. "You once admitted you were ruled too much by machines."

"I may have gone along with your way of thinking a few times for the fun of it, but I never lost sight of the real world. We're heading for a new century, Brit, and sooner or later machines will do nearly everything that's now done by hand."

Brit glared at him. "Then I can't imagine why you would want me to stay, now that Wonder Woman is finished. She should be able to answer your every need! Although you may have trouble teaching her to cuddle a crying child during a thunderstorm. Can a machine do that, Harrison?"

He greeted her outburst with a long moment of silence. "At least she won't lie to me," he said at last.

"I didn't lie—not exactly."

"All right, you didn't tell the whole truth. How could you do that, Brit? How could you make love to me in that bed and not tell me the real reason for coming to this house?"

"Because then I'd have to leave, just as I'm doing now!" Tears flooded her eyes and rolled down her cheeks as she grabbed the suitcase and the small computer.

"Let me carry—"

"I wouldn't consider your help," she said, lifting her quivering chin. "And as long as we're accusing each other, how could you make love to me in that bed, share what we've shared, and call it infatuation?"

"Brit, I—"

"You're like one of your machines. You know who you remind me of, Harrison? The Tin Man in *The Wizard of Oz.* No heart."

"That's ridiculous."

"Is it? You've turned yourself into a machine, and you expect me to be one, too. Handy to have around, but no feelings. Not that it matters anymore," she choked out. "Now that you've got your precious Wonder Woman, let her warm your bed!" Brit struggled out of the room with her belongings and thumped noisily up the stairs.

She heard Harrison's cry of protest, but when she stopped to catch her breath at the back door, she didn't hear his footsteps following her. And why should he stop her from leaving? After all, Brit had been right. His robot could give him everything except a woman's tenderness, and he didn't need that in his life. She blinked away her tears and fumbled in her purse for the car keys.

Harrison sat back on the bed and listened to the screech of Brit's car pulling out of the driveway.

176

When the noise died in the distance, he looked around the room. Her room—but not anymore.

He wandered into the tiny adjoining bath and flipped on the light, searching for something she might have left, something to give him an excuse to see her again. Nothing. The scent of her cologne hung in the air, and the towel was still damp from her last shower, but otherwise there was no evidence that she'd ever been there.

A haggard face stared back from the medicine cabinet mirror, and Harrison rubbed his hand absently across his prickly beard. He needed a shave. But he didn't have much reason to shave twice a day now. He wouldn't be kissing Brit. Brit, who had wormed her way into his house and his heart and then admitted she'd only been there to spy on his robot. God, how that hurt! But of course it shouldn't hurt. The Tin Man didn't have any feelings.

Turning off the bathroom light, he returned to the bedroom and picked up the bottle of champagne. Time to celebrate. He laughed bitterly. The Tin Man would get well oiled.

Carelessly he tipped the bottle and splashed the liquid into one of the glasses. Some drops of champagne splattered out and ran down the goblet like shining tears. Her tears. He brought the dripping glass to his lips and drank thirstily.

If only he could invent the perfect woman, he thought, wiping his mouth with the back of his hand. First of all, she would have fine, light-colored hair that curved just under her jawline and sifted through his fingers like strands of silk.

He drained his goblet and watched the bubbles dance crazily as he refilled it. The perfect woman for him, he decided, would have wide-set, intelligent eyes and a mouth that was soft and firm at the same time, a mouth made for his kisses. She would have breasts that lifted for his touch, hips that curved beneath his palm when he—oh, hell, who was he kidding? She'd be exactly like Brit McIver.

He swallowed the last of the champagne in his glass and reached for the bottle again, wishing he could reach for Brit instead. He wanted her here now, wanted to taste the champagne on her lips before moving down to kiss the velvet softness of her breasts. Her heart would beat a rapid tattoo as he caressed her, and then . . .

With an agonized groan Harrison hurled his glass across the room. He watched it shatter against the wall before throwing himself onto the bed and burying his face in the pillow that still carried a hint of her elusive, maddeningly erotic scent. Unfortunately, Brit was wrong. The Tin Man had feelings.

For the next few days Brit ignored Riley's questions and concentrated on her business. Many of her other clients had been neglected during her stay at the Kent household, and Brit vowed to mend all her fences in preparation for the coming of Harrison Kent's Wonder Woman.

With all the clients she contacted, Brit emphasized the personal nature of her service and suggested new ways the Quintessential Woman might enhance their lives. She expanded her horizons, offering a masseuse for relaxing backrubs and a pet

178

lover to pamper and stroke neglected dogs and cats. She employed a home decorating expert whose specialty was the use of colors to improve the mood and disposition of family members. Every innovation Brit conceived was based on what she believed Wonder Woman could not do.

Late at night, when she could no longer make telephone calls, Brit planned her advertising strategy. Somewhere she'd find a photograph of a mechanical hand and contrast it with a picture of a human hand. She'd rent billboard space and maybe even a short spot on television to demonstrate the inadequacies of a machine when it came to providing the human touch. No matter what Harrison said, there were some things a robot couldn't do, and she'd prove it to her customers!

She slept little because sleep brought dreams, haunting pictures of the life she'd so abruptly left. Little Avery would appear, her blue eyes filled with tears at the terror of a thunderstorm. Then came John, struggling to find his pet mouse that had escaped once again. And then Shane, trying to be brave as a stranger took him to the emergency room with another injury.

But most of all, Brit dreamed of Harrison. Sometimes his boyish laughter would echo through the night air, but more often his words of passion would whisper through her mind and she would awake with a start, aching with the memory of strong arms that held her and hands that worked magic on her heated body. In the darkness Brit could still see his gaze, so full of desire that came perilously close to love.

179

Then she'd shake herself back to reality. She'd imagined love reflected in his eyes because that's what she had wanted there. To keep her sanity she had to remind herself that he refused to speak the word. *Infatuation* was what he'd called the emotion he felt. A dry chuckle escaped Brit's throat. Infatuation.

A knock on the apartment door in the middle of the morning caught Brit by surprise. Only her employees knew where she lived, she thought, getting up from the desk in the living room where she'd been working on the following week's schedule. Sticking her pen behind her ear, she padded barefoot to the door.

Brit hoped one of her retirees wasn't outside with a resignation in hand. The new regime would require more work, she'd warned them, but nobody had voiced any objections at her last employee meeting. Maybe Phillipe wanted to share a new recipe discovery, she mused, opening the door with an optimistic smile.

Her smile disappeared at the sight of the tall, dark-haired man standing in the hall with a small portfolio under one arm.

"Hello, Brit."

She couldn't make any words come out of her constricted throat, so she tipped her head forward in greeting. His brown open-necked shirt and gray sport coat didn't blend very well, but they covered the same appealing broad shoulders. His shadowed jaw still tempted her to touch its roughness, and his firm lips still reminded her of shared kisses and delirious moments of abandon.

But behind the silver rim of his glasses, his eyes looked tired. She squelched the compassion that welled up in her. He shouldn't be tired or dressed in mismatched clothes; he had Wonder Woman to take care of everything!

"I, ah, have the papers for John's name change. Technically I'm the only one who needs to sign them, but John insisted on your signature, too, considering your part in the whole project. I promised him I'd ask you to sign."

"Oh." And she'd imagined for a fraction of a second that he was here for some avowal of love or some remorseful speech about being sorry for all that had happened. Hah. "Won't you come in?"

"Thank you."

Her traitorous nose recorded the familiar scent of him as he passed by, and her body registered an immediate reaction. Damn her casual decision this morning to forgo a bra! If he looked closely, he could see her nipples pucker under the pale sweater.

And he was looking closely.

"Are the other two remembering to call John by his new name?" she asked, crossing her arms protectively over her chest.

"Yes." The word came out almost as a sigh.

"So where are these papers?" She tapped her foot impatiently, but without shoes the gesture had little effect other than a soft whispering noise against the carpet.

Harrison glanced down at her feet and smiled. "You never walked around our house barefoot."

"That would have looked very unprofessional. At

181

home I can afford to relax because my clients don't come here. Except for you, that is."

"I don't consider myself a client anymore."

"No, I guess you're not," she said brusquely, sitting at the desk and clearing a space for the documents he gave her. "Where do I sign?"

"Right there. Next to me."

The words were innocently spoken, she was sure, but as Harrison leaned over to point out the spot, Brit held her breath. How she longed to be next to him, sharing his days, filling his nights with love! Pushing aside her futile fantasies, she looked around for her pen.

"Right here, Brit." The fingers that had once brought her to the heights of ecstasy removed the pen from behind her ear and handed it to her.

His touch made her quiver with unquenched desire. Why did he have to be so sexy? Brit gripped the pen tightly and forced her attention to the paper in front of her.

She was concentrating so hard on signing her name without botching the job that she didn't see the little metal figure until it marched across the page and nearly fell into her lap.

The pen clattered to the desktop as she caught the whirring windup toy and gave Harrison a look of surprise.

He shrugged and grinned nervously. "Mikey the Miniature Messenger," he said as the toy's churning legs gradually stopped flailing the air.

Brit studied the little figure in her hand more carefully. A note was taped to his chest. With trembling fingers she pulled the note free. Underneath

182

the paper, painted on the gray metal of the mechanical toy, was a candy-red heart. Her eyes filled with unshed tears, she glanced up questioningly at Harrison.

"Read the note," he said gently.

She put down the toy and opened the piece of paper.

> *Dear Quintessential Woman,*
> *Machines are wonderful, but you're right. They have no heart. In your absence I've discovered that I do, and it's breaking. Please come back. I love you.*
> *The Tin Man.*

The tears spilled unheeded from her eyes as she lifted her gaze from the note.

"John didn't really insist on your signature, although he liked the idea," Harrison admitted.

"You used the signature as an excuse to come over here?" she murmured, hardly able to speak around the lump in her throat.

He nodded. "I had to see you again, but I was afraid you wouldn't let me in unless it had something to do with the kids. I used your feelings for them, Brit. I would have used anything. I—"

The paralysis left Brit's legs, and she hurled herself out of the chair and into his arms. "Yes, say it!" she cried, taking his face in both hands.

His arms were trembling as they tightened around her. His dark gaze moved slowly over her upturned face and finally looked deep into her eyes. "I love you, Brit."

The sigh that escaped her lips came from the depths of her soul. "And I love you, Tin Man."

At the sound of papers rustling to the floor, Brit put down her book and glanced across her pillow at Harrison. The schematic drawing he'd been studying had slipped from his limp grasp, and his chest rose and fell in regular, shallow breaths. He was asleep.

Brit reached for the panel of buttons beside the bed and pushed the red one. "Lock up the house and make the coffee, Wonder Woman," she said into the intercom.

"Yes, ma'am," came the melodious reply.

"And wake us at six thirty. Wake the children at seven."

"Yes, ma'am."

Brit smiled and shook her head. She still wasn't quite used to giving verbal instructions to a machine, even after all these weeks. Aiming for another button, Brit shut off the reading lamps. Her hand hovered over the Glo-Ball on her bedside table, and on an impulse she rested her palm on it, bringing the soft light to life.

In the gentle illumination from the Glo-Ball, she leaned her chin on her hands and gazed at the sleeping, beard-roughened face of her husband. She marveled at the depth of her love, at the passion that grew stronger with each magic moment that they lay in each other's arms. Just watching him sleep aroused her. He'd climbed into bed naked, but the papers in his hand had told her he wanted to get a little more work done, so she hadn't disturbed him.

Carefully she removed his glasses and put them on the table next to him where he would find them when he awoke. Tomorrow was a big day, and neither of them could afford to waste any time. But tonight . . . Desire fought with reason as Brit's attention focused on the sensuous curve of his lower lip.

Desire won. She pulled open the drawer of her bedside table and took out a small metal object. Winding the key on the back of the tiny toy, she set the whirring figure on Harrison's chest. Stiffly the little man marched through the jungle of dark hair until Harrison sat bolt upright and the toy tumbled to the floor.

"What the hell was that?"

Brit smiled. "Mikey the Miniature Messenger."

"Oh, yeah?" Harrison's sleep-glazed eyes cleared as he caught sight of Brit's negligee-clad body. "Were you wearing that sexy little number when I came to bed?"

"Yep."

"Did I have my glasses on?"

"Yep."

He shook his head. "I must be losing it."

"You had the schematic to work on. I understand."

He reached for her. "Next time don't be so damned understanding," he murmured, burying his face against her neck. "I don't want to miss stuff like this. Mm. It comes off easy, too."

"That's because I'm so obliging," Brit whispered, lifting her hips as he swept the negligée away.

"Oh, sweetheart, are you ever," he groaned, stroking the satin smoothness of her inner thigh.

Brit gloried in the scratch of his beard as he suckled her breasts and transformed her nipples to aching points of pleasure. His exploring hand moved between her thighs, and she felt his shudder of eagerness at discovering that she was already drenched with excitement.

"Thank Mikey for me," he whispered against her ear as he moved over her.

She rose to meet his purposeful thrust and uttered a whimper of delight at their joining.

"I'll never get enough of you," he rumbled. "God, you feel good."

"And you feel . . . fantastic," she said breathlessly as he rocked forward, putting pressure on her most sensitive spot.

"I'm going to make this last all night," he promised, initiating a lazy rhythm.

"Sure you are," she murmured. She knew well that neither of them had much luck keeping their intense passion in check. But they had fun trying.

"Oh, Brit," he sighed, giving in to the frantic urgings of his body and increasing the tempo.

"Never mind," she moaned, wanting the bolder movements as much as he. "Just . . . love me."

His voice was hoarse. "I do. More than life," he gasped. "Brit . . . Brit!"

She tightened her grip on his back as the world began to spin out of control. Gladly she allowed herself to be taken to a realm of pure sensation and blinding love, a world where their mingled cries bore eloquent testimony to their joy in each other.

The descent back to reality seemed to take a long time, and Harrison lay still, not wanting to leave her delicious warmth. "How can this keep getting better?" he murmured into her hair.

Brit nuzzled his ear. "You're the scientist. You tell me."

"What happens between us in this bed defies scientific explanation."

"Then it must be a miracle."

"Guess so." He kissed the side of her neck and inhaled her wonderful scent.

"I'm glad I woke you."

"Me, too."

"Now I feel ready for tomorrow."

He propped his head on his fist and gazed down at her. "Nervous?"

"A little. After all, it's my first demonstration of a domestic robot."

"You'll be fine. After all, she's just a machine. You're the original Quintessential Woman, and that's worth more than a million mechanical wonders."

"You're so perceptive, Mr. Kent."

"You're so receptive, Mrs. Kent." He stroked the curve of her hip lovingly. "You know, Brit, for two intelligent people, we sure are dumb. Why did it take the kids to suggest combining my domestic robots with your home management service?"

"Kids are smart and people in love can be very dumb, Harrison."

"I think the word is *stubborn*. Thank God for those kids. They were motivated to find a way to bring us back together, though. They missed you like crazy, and I was impossible to live with. They probably dreamed up the idea out of self-defense."

Brit chuckled. "Probably. By the way, Riley called today. She's leaving for Seattle next week."

"Did she find an office partner out there?"

"Yes, and he's perfect. An accountant. She read me his letter, which he addressed to 'Mr. Dugan.' Riley decided not to disabuse him of the idea that she's a man. I'd love to be there when she prances in wearing a pair of those stiletto heels."

Harrison grinned. "So would I." He outlined Brit's kiss-swollen lips with the tip of his finger. "But not really. I wouldn't want to be anywhere except right here with you."

She nibbled on the end of his finger. "And I want to be right here with you, Tin Man."

"That's very erotic, Brit." His breathing quickened as she took his finger into her mouth. "You may be ready for tomorrow, but I think I need another dose of encouragement."

She felt him stir within her, and fresh desire welled up, demanding expression. She squirmed beneath him impatiently.

Laughing, he took his damp finger from her mouth and trailed it between her breasts. "You wanton wench. I think you'll go along with the idea."

She smiled provocatively. "I might."

"And that's why," he murmured as his lips hovered above hers, "you'll always be my Quintessential Woman."